LANCASTER COUNTY SECOND CHANCES 5

RUTH PRICE

ISBN:1515376079
ISBN-13:9781515376071

TABLE OF CONTENTS

ACKNOWLEDGMENTS

All Praise first to the Almighty God who has given me this wonderful opportunity to share my words and stories with the world. Next, I have to thank my family, especially my husband Harold who supports me even when I am being extremely crabby. Further, I have to thank my wonderful friends and associates with Global Grafx Press who support me in every way as a writer. Lastly, I wouldn't be able to do any of this without you, my readers. I hold you in my heart and prayers and hope that you enjoy my books.

All the best and Blessings,

Ruth.

CHAPTER ONE

Isaac Muller staggered back against the workshop door. Leah Hauser pressed her barely clothed body right into his and brushed her lips across his neck. The touch of Leah's tongue on his skin sent crazy electricity branching deep through his body.

Isaac's mind blanked out. That instant, Leah's supple body and exploratory kisses were the only things in it. She was begging him for pleasure, murmuring obscenities, raking his back like a clawing cat.

Isaac closed his eyes and let that split-second of insanity reel out. Leah's hands moved down his chest, fretting the flimsy belt that kept his robe around his body. Another instant, and his robe would be on the floor, they would both be naked, and it would be too late to turn back.

But though his mind was stunned, Isaac's heart revived. The thought of Cora flared in the darkness and flowered into a thousand bright memories.

He imagined Cora's beautiful blue eyes—but now the sweet, trusting look that he loved was gone. In its place was the dull, dead look of disillusionment and betrayal.

He had only an instant to decide.

Isaac pulled his mouth away.

***

He clamped his hands around Leah's shoulders and thrust her firmly out from him. "Go *back to the house*, Leah," he said sternly. "I told you that I'm a married man. A *happily married man.*"

Even though Isaac had only used a fraction of his strength, Leah stumbled violently backwards and only saved herself from falling by grabbing at the work table.

"Go away and stop following me," he panted. "*Find a man of your own.*"

Leah leaned heavily against the work table. Gradually she gathered her robe, and her composure.

"Your mouth says one thing, Isaac Muller," she replied breathlessly. "But your *body* says another. I know you can't admit it, even to yourself, but *you want me.*

"That bride of yours will drag you down. What kind of life can you make for yourself here, with *Cora Lapp*? She's a train wreck, Isaac. She'll ruin whatever you try to build.

"Sooner or later you'll see that you married the wrong woman. It might not be tonight. *But you'll come to me, Isaac.*

"And I'll be waiting."

Isaac made a tired, waving motion with one hand. "Go back to the house, Leah," he murmured, and turned into the little bedroom. He closed the door behind him and turned the lock.

He could hear Leah crying softly on the other side of the door for a few minutes, and then the sound of the outer door closing announced that she had given up at last.

But Isaac sat in the dark, wide-eyed and panting, for a long time.

Then he gathered his wits, dressed, and packed.

***

It was deep night when Isaac emerged from the little shop bedroom. He walked across the yard, to Levi Hauser's front porch, and slipped a small handwritten note under the door.

Words of apology, of a family crisis, of the need to break off their contract. He would think of the details later.

The important thing was to put as much distance between himself and Leah as he could.

The moon was high and bright in the sky, and a chill mist was rising from the meadows. It was almost ten miles back to town, and it was going to be a long, cold walk.

But staying in that cramped, tiny shop was impossible now.

Isaac shook his head. One minute, he was sleeping peacefully in his bed – the next, Leah Hauser was plastered over his chest and doing her best to untie his robe.

He wondered if it was real, or if he was still dreaming. But the rocky road underneath his feet and the cold night air were real enough.

It had all happened so *fast*.

Isaac pulled his mouth into a tight line. Leah had ambushed him when he was half-asleep. She had been calculating, dishonest. For an instant he was angry, but the feeling quickly faded.

It was useless to be angry at Leah.

He was the one who had really failed. He should've told Leah long ago that he had no feelings for her. She had clearly been confused by his silence.

It was painful to admit, but looking back, he *had* been flattered to have two beautiful women like Cora and Leah fighting for his attention. Whenever he had been worried about losing Cora, all he had to do was remember how she looked when Leah Hauser even *talked* to him, and he had been comforted.

When they'd quarreled during their courtship, he had once tried to make Cora jealous by encouraging Leah. And it had worked too well. Cora had overreacted in fear and anger and now Leah was bitter and full of revenge.

He had been wrong to do it, and now he was paying a price.

It was *his* fault, really.

A full-body wave of shame surged up from Isaac's feet to his hair. He wondered why he'd hesitated -- why he'd allowed Leah to crawl over him.

Now, under the cool, sane night sky, he was shaken to think that he'd been *seconds* from destroying everything he loved.

It was going to be hard to meet Cora's eyes, once he got home. He had let Leah pin him against the door, and kiss him, and if he hadn't come to his senses quickly, he would this minute be lying in the dark, wrestling with bitter regret.

He set his jaw. He'd have to tell Cora, tell her *everything*, to preserve his own self-respect, and her trust. But nothing would hurt her more than knowing that he had allowed Leah Hauser to...

He imagined the look in her eyes, and quick tears sprang to his own. Cora was the last person on earth he would ever want to hurt -- but that was *exactly* what was about to happen.

She had tried to warn him, even begged him not to go to the Hauser's. But he hadn't been willing to listen. Now he wished that he *had*.

An owl called in the meadow off to the right of the road. Farther off, its mate replied.

Isaac transferred his tool bag from one arm to the other, and trudged doggedly along the road, praying that when he got back home, Cora would still be there... and that she would still be with him, after she found out what had just happened.

CHAPTER TWO

A faint predawn pink filled the sky when Isaac finally arrived in the deserted town. A solitary dog barking was the only sound as he dragged himself up the steps to the little apartment. He opened the door, dropped his tools on the floor, and stumbled to the bedroom in exhaustion.

But when he opened the door, his heart sank. Their bed was perfectly made -- and empty.

Cora was gone.

Isaac collapsed across the quilt. The thought came to him that he would have to get up, and go find her. He reached out to brace himself against the mattress but his fingers unfurled on the coverlet.

It was his last conscious action before sleep closed its arms over him.

***

"Cora. *Cora.*"

The midnight sky overhead was white with stars, and the moon was bright enough to see by. He was waiting for Cora by the creek, just below his father's farm. There was no sign of her.

He climbed over the little fence, skipped over the creek, and sat down on the tree branch where they always talked as children. He resigned himself to a long wait: sometimes it took a while for her to be able to slip away.

The creek whispered to itself in the darkness, and he rubbed his arms. It was getting chilly, but he would have waited all night.

Guilt stabbed him. He kept coming back, and back, but they shouldn't be meeting this way. They were taking a crazy risk, but he couldn't bear to be…

A low sound, hardly more distinct than the murmuring of the brook, broke into his thoughts. He turned to listen: it was coming from the Lapp's, somewhere on the other side of the hill.

He stepped down from the limb and climbed the steep rise. To his surprise, the sound he heard was Cora's voice. She was answered by a man, a voice he didn't recognize.

They were both speaking softly, but to his alarm, they both sounded agitated.

Cora suddenly screamed -- a ragged, anguished sound that made the hairs on his neck stand up. He broke into a run, and when he topped the rise, he jolted to a stop.

Cora was lying on the ground, struggling against a stranger who had his hands *around her neck.*

He felt as if he'd been struck by lightning.

He didn't know how they got there, but suddenly his hands were around the man's chest. He yanked him up in a high, wide arc through the air, and then slammed him against the ground. He left the stranger writhing there without a backward glance and scrambled to where Cora was lying.

She was looking up at the sky like a beautiful, broken doll, and horror thrilled through every vein in his body. He grasped her hand. It was lifeless.

"Cora? Cora? Cora?"

***

He moaned, turned his head restlessly. The dream shifted.

Cora raised her chin and looked up at him. The firelight in the little bedroom flickered in her eyes, turned her hair to gold. She caressed his face with her hand.

"I always imagined how this would be," she whispered. "It's better even than I dreamed, Isaac."

Her eyes were full of – he couldn't name it – something

that energized and terrified him. That sweet, trusting, *hero worship* look. Like she would never entertain a bad thought about him.

That look he loved, and worried about.

She kissed him, and he took her in his arms again, and she opened up to him as sweetly and softly as a flower opening to the sun. It was like dying, being loved like that: the whole of his life was divided into before, and after.

He had thought that he loved her, but he was wrong.

He had no idea, before then, how fierce and terrifying love was. How sweet, and how like fire.

He had buried his face in her hair, breathing in the sweet scent of it, moving his cheek across her shoulder, luxuriating in how smooth it was against his skin.

"Cora."

***

He moved his lips soundlessly.

They were sitting at the kitchen table now, and she was looking at him as if she expected him to take her over his knee.

"Now I am going to get rid of the cell phone," he was telling her, "and we will never speak of it again."

Her eyes had been like big blue marbles, pleading with him like a child's. He had to break the little phone in two, but it had felt cruel, and he had to remind himself why he was doing it, why it was necessary.

He wanted to spoil her, even though that was not the Amish way.

It had gone to his heart, her downturned mouth: but this much wisdom he had learned, that he would be better off if Cora never suspected that.

She had mumbled to herself, and pouted for a little while.

"*I heard that, Cora.*"

But that night, she had snuggled into his arms and begged for a kiss, and he had been glad to give her as many of *those* as she wanted.

***

The dream changed again. He frowned; his hands clenched and unclenched.

"I have something to tell, you, Cora."

Cora had returned home. He sat down on the sofa and motioned for her to sit down beside him. She came and sat down expectantly, smiling, watching him with innocent eyes. She had no reason to expect anything bad.

He turned his head restlessly on the coverlet.

"I should have listened to you, Cora, when you asked me not to go to the Hauser's," he was saying. "Because something happened that you need to know about."

He watched her eyes darken with worry. She took his hand.

"What, Isaac? What happened?"

He tossed his head on the quilt, and his eyes rolled under their closed lids.

"Leah Hauser tried to – she came to –"

He watched in dread as the truth dawned in her eyes, and chased that trusting, happy look away – forever.

"Oh, no, *Isaac*."

She pulled her hand out of his.

"Cora, nothing happened beyond that she kissed me, and, and--"

Cora's face crumpled into grief. She jumped up, sobbing, and ran into the bedroom, slamming the door behind her. He pressed up against it, knocking urgently on the door.

"Cora! Cora, *listen to me!*"

He moaned and thrashed on the bed.

"Cora…"

But it was all fading away now, even Cora's sobs. He

pressed his cheek against the door, but to his confusion, it felt soft, and smelled like lavender.

His eyes fluttered open. Slowly it came to him: *It had been a dream*. Isaac pulled his hands down over his face and sighed in relief.

He struggled up on one elbow and squinted at the window. The sunlight outside announced that he had slept the day away: it was now late afternoon.

But to his confusion, *one* part of his dream lingered. There was a soft, persistent knocking at the front door.

CHAPTER THREE

Isaac rolled out of bed and hurried to the front door, but when he pulled it open, it was not Cora's pert face that greeted him.

Joseph Lapp blocked out the light in his doorway. Joseph was in shadow as well: his startling eyes had darkened to a gunmetal gray.

"May I come in, Isaac?" he asked.

Isaac ran a hand through his mop of hair. He was surprised, and not all that pleased: Joseph was the last person he had expected to see.

But he nodded.

Joseph came in slowly and silently. When Isaac gestured to the sofa, he sat down on it stiffly.

Isaac lowered himself into a chair and faced his brother-in-law. He was in no mood for formalities, and they wouldn't have done much good, anyway.

So he got right to the point.

"Is Cora staying with you?"

Joseph nodded.

Isaac bit his lip. "Is she – is she all right?"

Joseph raised tired eyes. "She's upset. She says the two of you quarreled. And that you were working at Levi Hauser's."

Isaac stood up. "I'll come and get her."

Joseph didn't follow. "Let's talk a while first, Isaac," he suggested. He looked down at his hands and sighed.

"You were at the Hauser's for a little over a week, I think. Cora came to us on the first night."

Isaac looked away, and nodded. "We did quarrel," he confessed. "I was laid off from the shop, and I haven't been able to find work. Levi Hauser offered me work, and I told Cora I was going to take the job. She didn't want me to take it, because –"

He went red, and broke off. "Anyway, she was upset. But there's no reason to be, anymore. I stopped working there."

"I'm not here to get in your business," Joseph told him carefully. "I came here because Cora is *inconsolable*. She seems to think that you're *very* angry with her."

Isaac looked down at his feet. "I'm not angry with her," he replied quietly.

"I didn't think that sounded right, either," Joseph answered, "but she seems to be convinced that the two of you are on the brink of divorce."

Isaac looked up sharply. "Is that what *she* told you?"

"It's what she fears."

Isaac shook his head in consternation. "I never suggested any such thing," he frowned, "I never even *thought* it! But – I *did* say some things to her that I shouldn't have said. I regret them now. Is… Cora angry?"

Joseph shook his head. "No. Cora is *terrified.*"

Isaac frowned.

"Of *me*?"

"Of losing you."

Isaac shook his head and sighed. "I – I was *harsh* with Cora," he admitted softly. "I've been out of my mind with worry these last few weeks. I finally got a little work, and she didn't want me to take the job."

He lowered his head. "But there was more to it than just that."

Joseph watched him, and said nothing.

"You were right, Joseph," Isaac admitted, in a low voice. "I didn't see it at first, but you were right. I didn't make Cora feel safe to tell me what she thought, and so – she hid something from me, again, and when I found out, I got upset. But she didn't mean any harm. She *never* means any harm. It was my fault.

"I was – I was scared, I guess. It felt like she didn't trust me anymore. Like she didn't think I was a good provider. I was afraid she'd lost *respect* for me."

Joseph shook his head, and seemed to repress an exasperated exclamation by force of will.

"Isaac, I am Cora's brother. She has told me things that she may not even have told you. I promise you, Cora is beyond all reason where you are concerned. She has proved it *over and over*," he added dryly.

"Yes, everything's all right for now," Isaac broke out impatiently, "but if this goes on, who knows." He looked out the window.

Joseph considered him in silence for a long while. At last he coughed, and looked down at the floor, and up at the ceiling.

"Have you thought about starting your own business, Isaac?"

Isaac shrugged. "It costs money to start a business," he replied. "I'll have to get a job before I can even think about that."

"You have a real gift for woodworking. What if you rented

this whole house, instead of just the second floor, and used the lower half to sell your own furniture? You might even work in partnership with Gideon Miller. You could refer your customers to him for cabinets, and he could refer his customers to you for furnishings."

Isaac pressed his mouth into a line. "It sounds good, but I told you, I don't have the money."

"What if I loaned you the money?"

Isaac looked up sharply and went beet red. "I don't want money from my wife's family," he stated flatly.

"I'm not offering you a *gift*," Joseph replied evenly. "I'm offering you a loan, at the going rate. No special favors."

Isaac said nothing, and Joseph shrugged. "Think about it, anyway. Take your time."

"I will," Isaac mumbled. "Thank you, Joseph."

Then he stood up. "It's time for Cora to come home. I'll come and get her now."

Joseph didn't follow.

"There's more, Isaac."

***

Joseph's grim expression made Isaac slowly sink back down into his chair.

"Mary Stoltzfus – you remember her? -- ran away to Europe without telling anybody. She came back while you were at the Hauser farm.

"Mary came back looking like – well, you'll see her soon enough. She cut her hair and painted her face and bought a lot of English clothes. So the bishop's wife called a meeting of the school board and they came over to Fannie's house to tell Mary that she couldn't teach at the school any more unless she repented. Both Mary *and Cora* were called to the meeting."

Isaac's eyes widened.

"When Cora saw that Mary was going to be fired for dressing English, she told the board members that it was *her* fault, and not Mary's. She told them that *she'd* encouraged Mary to dress English, and that she had her own cell phone. Some silliness about a boy. It doesn't matter now."

Joseph sighed. "Now they're *both* barred from teaching. Mary's in the clear apart from that, since she hasn't joined the church. But Cora –"

Isaac groaned and put his face in his hands.

"Of course I can't let her take the blame alone," Joseph went on. "I was the one who gave her the phone. Katie and I have talked about it, and I'll confess my part to the bishop."

Isaac nodded wordlessly.

"Cora promises that she's going to repent for breaking the *Ordnung*, and that she'll say anything she needs to say. I can't see the bishop coming down hard on her, at least for a first offense. She confessed voluntarily, too. That should go in her favor.

"But getting in trouble with the elders is not what Cora most fears. Isaac –" Joseph looked up, and his eyes were piercing – "she is most afraid of *you*, or at least, of you being *angry*. She knows that you were angry before, and now she's terrified that this news will make that even worse. She didn't even have the courage to come back and face you herself.

"She wouldn't explain *why*, so I came here to tell you that if she has any *reason* to be afraid –"

Isaac looked startled. He shook his head vehemently. "No, *no*, I'm not angry," he said softly. "Even if I was, I could *never* –"

Joseph nodded slowly. "If I didn't know you as well as I do, Isaac Muller, I might not let you come get her."

He sighed. "But I *do* know you, and I also know Cora. She's amazingly silly at the best of times, and what little judgment she has, flies out the window whenever it's about *you*."

Isaac shot him a straight look, and replied shortly: "As long as she *is* with me, you don't ever have to be worried about Cora, Joseph."

Joseph nodded and rose. "All right then, Isaac. Let's go get her."

CHAPTER FOUR

Cora sat in the children's swing under the big oak tree in Joseph's back yard. Her gleaming hair flowed around her shoulders and rippled down her back like so many bright rivulets of water. The rays of the dying sun caught her, and painted her hair red-gold.

Her head drooped, and her hands held the swing loosely. Her eyes were on the ground, and her expression was one of gentle melancholy.

A faint footstep made her look up. Her sister-in-law Katie was standing there, watching her with sympathy in her eyes.

"I wish you would believe me," Katie said softly. "Everything is going to be all right."

"I wish I could be as sure as you are," Cora replied tonelessly.

Katie pulled out a brush and began working with Cora's

long hair. "I couldn't find the round one," she explained, pulling the bristles gently through the golden skeins. "But it doesn't matter. Your hair would look lovely no matter what you use on it."

The ghost of a smile played over Cora's lips. "Isn't that *hochmut*?" she teased, looking up at her sister in law.

"Maybe. But it's true just the same," Katie replied fondly. "Still, you need to get that beautiful hair of yours pinned up before Isaac gets here. You don't want to let him see you without your cap on."

"Thank you, Katie. I think it's dry enough now. I just wanted to look my best when he got here. I'd wear makeup like Mary, if it was allowed!"

She put her hand to her eyes, and Katie clucked her tongue.

"Now, no more of that! You don't want Isaac to see you with a red nose and eyes, do you?" she chided gently.

"No."

"Well, then."

She clipped a row of bobby pins to her apron and began methodically pinning Cora's hair. "It's normal to have some misunderstandings, especially when you're newlyweds. Joseph and I haven't always seen eye to eye. But we always come back together again, eventually."

"You're always so wise, Katie," Cora objected. "You've

never been in trouble. But I've ruined *everything*. Isaac tried so hard to keep me from messing up, but I messed up anyway. I wouldn't blame him if he never spoke to me again."

"You shouldn't fret. He may be upset temporarily, but it won't last."

"How do you know?" Cora asked wistfully.

"I know because Isaac loves you. He *has* always loved you, and he *will* always love you. If you can't see it, at least give the rest of us credit." She stepped back and inspected her handiwork.

"There, it's ready. Go ahead and put on your cap. I think that's Joseph and Isaac now."

Cora looked up quickly. Sure enough, two buggies were visible on the road in the distance. She shook out her white bonnet and placed it carefully over her hair while Katie pinned it in place.

Katie smiled, and turned to go, but Cora grabbed her hand.

"Don't leave me, Katie," she gasped, "I can't face Isaac. I'm afraid that he's going to – that he –"

Katie touched Cora's face and smiled sadly. "Cora, there's only one way to get over these fears. Talk to your husband."

"I'm just so afraid of losing him, Katie. If you could have seen how angry he was! Isaac is *never* angry!"

"*Talk to your husband*," Katie whispered. She gave Cora a peck on the cheek and walked slowly back to the house.

Cora watched her go with tears in her eyes. Then she turned a fearful glance to the road.

Joseph was already pulling into the barn and – their *own* buggy was still in the road. Isaac was just sitting in it, not moving.

She looked down at her feet.

She heard Joseph unhitching his horse, and leading it away to its stall. She heard him walking across the lawn and up the porch steps. She heard the sound of the screen door slamming behind him as he went inside.

And still there was silence. Cora felt her eyes tearing up again, and wiped them with one hand. She couldn't bring herself to look toward the road. The long minutes dragged out.

"Cora."

Finally Isaac was standing there. Her lip trembled, and she couldn't answer, couldn't look up.

"Cora, come home."

She looked up. Isaac towered over her. She couldn't see his face for her tears, but his voice was the voice she knew and loved – strong, gentle, and quiet.

"Please come home."

Cora's mouth crumpled. "Oh, Isaac!" she sobbed, and put her arms out like a child. Isaac lifted her up, and she flung her arms around his neck and buried her face in his chest. Her chest vibrated with sobs.

Isaac stared over her shoulder as if he saw something that frightened him. "There, now, my little bird," he murmured, "how could I have said such mean things. I'm sorry, Cora. I was angry, but I should never have been so harsh.

"Come home now, Cora. *It's time to come home.*"

But she hid her face in her hands. "Isaac, I'm the one who's sorry," she sobbed. "I've ruined *everything*, and I wouldn't blame you if you never –"

But Isaac gently peeled her hands away from her face and kissed her.

Cora received his kiss like a thirsty plant drinking water, and then rested her head on his shoulder. "I was so afraid that you'd be *angry*," she told him, squeezing her eyes together.

"I'm not angry, Cora," he told her. "Whatever we have to face, we'll face together."

She broke into fresh sobs. Isaac let her wind down, and then put an arm around her shoulder and walked her toward the buggy. He helped her up into the seat and climbed up into the buggy with her.

Once he was there, he leaned over and kissed her again for good measure -- slowly, roundly and gently.

Then he turned the horse's head toward town, and the buggy curved around in the road.

But as the buggy pulled away, Isaac looked back toward the house just in time to see Joseph turn away from the front door.

CHAPTER FIVE

"I tell you, Mamm, *it wasn't her fault.*"

Mary Stoltzfus looked up at her mother hopelessly. Ever since the school board ladies had left their home, her mother had been pounding her with lectures and warnings. Mary sighed. *Nothing* seemed to get through to her distracted mother: no explanations worked on her, and she entertained no appeals. Even *logic* didn't seem to matter.

Mary looked up grimly, thinking that her mother seemed to be running on pure adrenalin.

Fannie sniffed into a handkerchief. "I trusted Cora Lapp. I gave her a chance when no one else would. And this is how she repays me!"

"You were right to give her the job," Mary pleaded. "Cora turned out to be a *wonderful* teacher."

"She betrayed my trust!" Fannie's lip quivered.

"Mamm, listen to me. Cora is *not* to blame for me going to Paris. I've been dreaming about it for *years*, long before she and I became friends. I would have done it sooner or later, even if I'd never met her."

Fannie gave her daughter a wounded look. "And I suppose you chose to dress – *like this* –" she gestured to Mary's form-fitting top and jeans – "all on your own, as well?"

"Cora only gave me the clothes catalogs to encourage me to dress nice for Seth Troyer. She was always trying *something* to get the two of us together. That was the only reason she gave me the catalog. *And* the only reason she used the phone. She wanted me to *talk to Seth*."

"And actually, it *worked*," she added, almost to herself. "I *did* call him, once or twice."

Fannie seemed slightly mollified. "Well, if you're *finally* seeing sense about that fine, upstanding boy, I won't discourage you, Mary, but it was still wrong of Cora to tempt you with things that are against the *Ordnung*. I know you haven't joined the church, and that you're still on your *rumspringa*. But you've gone *far* beyond what anyone imagined! When I think of you all alone, out among the English, and in a *foreign country* –"

Mary took her mother's hands. "Mamm, it was *amazing*," she pleaded. "It was the best week of my *life*."

Fannie stared at her in consternation. "You're *Amish*,

Mary," she said quietly. "You belong *here*, with your *family*. Not in some strange English city, across the ocean!"

She tossed her head and looked away. "And I suppose, if Cora Muller was doing something to encourage you to stay *here*, instead of doing *that* then I can forgive her."

Mary looked down, and sighed. But she only said: "I'm glad, Mamm." She kissed her mother's cheek. "Cora really *is* a good person. She was just trying to get me to – to look at Seth in a different light."

"And so you should!" her mother retorted. She dabbed at her eyes again. "Oh, Mary, I don't know whether I'm going or coming. I've lost both you and Cora at the school, your *awful* hair is the talk of the county. Thank heaven you haven't yet joined the church. At least we don't have to worry about you being shunned!

"But decent people are still going to wonder about you, Mary," Fannie told her solemnly. "Anyone who hadn't seen you for a while would think you were English! You look so odd!

"And what are you going to do for work, while you're not teaching?"

Mary looked down at her hands. "I'm sorry about that for your sake, Mamm," she replied quietly. "I'll have to look for work someplace else – at least, in the short term."

Fannie gripped her arms. "Mary, grow your hair back out,"

she urged, "go back to dressing the way that you *should*, and maybe they'll let you come back to school in the fall."

"I *like* dressing this way, Mamm," Mary replied.

Her mother turned away from her. "Oh, Mary, I don't know what to do with you anymore," she cried. "Go, go out and do your chores, so I can rest. I have a splitting headache -- worrying about you!"

Mary sighed, and nodded, and walked out past her mother, across the living room, and out the front door.

***

It was a beautiful spring morning, bright and cool and fresh.

Mary took a deep breath. It was a relief to be out of the house.

She picked up a little trowel, and basket of bulbs, and walked out into the garden at the side of the house. She tossed the basket on the ground and knelt down beside it.

Her home, her parent's farm, the whole county, was as beautiful as a post card. The trees swayed softly in a light breeze, birds fluttered from branch to branch, and the only sound on the wind was the faint sound of a cow lowing from a far pasture.

When she raised her eyes, soft, rolling green countryside

was the only thing that she could see, all the way to the horizon.

It really was idyllic, but the sight of it made her almost sad.

Her childhood home already felt like the past.

Mary took the trowel and stabbed a hole in the soft garden earth. She plopped a fat bulb down into the gash and covered it over with earth.

She had returned from the outside world only bodily. She had longed for it every waking moment, and when she fell asleep, she dreamed of it.

She stabbed the ground again with the trowel.

She was never going to teach at the school again. She was never going to go back to dressing Amish, and she was never going to grow out her hair.

Last week, in Paris, she had *decided*.

It hurt her to think of the pain that decision was going to bring to her parents. They were going to be *devastated*.

Mary carved out another gash in the earth.

But the only thing that would ever make them happy was for her to stay here for the rest of her life.

And that was unthinkable, now.

She clapped the dirt off of her hands and wiped her brow

with one elbow. She had no idea how to be English, not yet. She only had a few jeans and tees, a short haircut, and a nice dress.

She didn't know how to *do* anything, except teach, and the rules for English teachers were very different.

Mary looked wistfully out across the rolling fields. She didn't know how to be anything but a gangly, bookish Amish girl.

But she was sure of one thing: She was going to do whatever it took to learn.

CHAPTER SIX

Mary stood up and looked out across the fields. A faint sound was gradually gaining strength. It was the sound of an approaching buggy. She stood up with her empty basket and walked around to the front yard.

She was just in time to see Seth Troyer pull up in the road outside their front yard. He was looking pleased with himself -- she supposed, because for once in his life, he had scored some wheels.

He cracked a wide, white grin and gestured to the rig.

"Care to go for a ride?" he asked.

Mary glanced back over her shoulder at the house, and then looked at Seth.

"Sure, why not."

She dropped the basket and climbed up into the buggy with him. Seth flicked the reins, and the horse broke into a trot.

"It's a fine day for driving," Seth told her. "Especially with such a beautiful woman!"

Mary twisted her mouth. "Don't mess with me, Seth," she warned him. "I'm not in the mood."

"I meant every word," Seth told her cheerfully. "I *really* like your new look. You look sophisticated, and a little --" his eyes widened – "*dangerous*."

Mary turned her eyes to the passing countryside. "You may be right. If you keep it up, I may push you out of the buggy."

Seth behaved as if he hadn't heard her. "I thought you might want to get out of the house for a while," he said. "I understand how it is. It's hard sometimes, to be a *progressiv*e."

Mary shrugged, and looked down at her hands.

"Do you know Weeping Rock?" Seth asked.

Mary nodded.

"We're going there," Seth informed her. "I have a picnic basket in the back seat. It has French cheese and red grapes and baguettes and a bottle of genuine *champagne*."

Mary looked over at Seth. And for the first time since she had known him, he didn't look like a geek.

She reached for his hand and gave it a grateful squeeze.

"Thanks, Seth," she said softly. "That's really nice of you."

***

Weeping Rock was an outcrop of stone deep in the woods. It got its name from the network of little silver rivulets that trickled over its edge and formed a small, clear pool at its base. It was one of the better-known lover's lanes in the district, and when they arrived, it was temporarily available.

Seth climbed out of the buggy and held out a hand for Mary. She let him help her down, and they found a nice spot near the pool to spread the blanket that Seth had brought.

Mary looked down at the lunch he was unpacking on the red blanket.

"You think of everything, don't you, Seth?" she marveled.

He was setting out plates – *china* plates – champagne glasses, bowls for fruit, and a cooler full of ice for the wine bottle. Next came boxes and boxes of store-bought delicacies that took her right back to her hotel room in Paris – goose liver pate, éclairs, little gourmet crackers, handmade cheese, little watercress and cucumber sandwiches, chicken salad with pecans, cold roast beef and chicken, and chocolate cake.

He grinned at her with those white teeth, and to Mary's alarm, something strange happened to her eyes. *Something,* she didn't know what, was lifted clean away from them, and by some trick of the dappled light –

Seth Troyer was suddenly a handsome boy.

She gaped at him, tucked a strand of hair nervously behind her ear, and sat down on the blanket.

Seth handed her a glass and uncorked the bottle with a loud *pop.*

"I guess this won't be like what you had in Paris," he smiled, pouring it into her glass, "but the man at the shop told me it was supposed to be good."

Mary took an appreciative sip. The little bubbles were just like she remembered.

"Seth, I don't know what to say," she told him. "You shouldn't have gone to all this trouble."

"I was glad to do it," he told her, filling his own glass. "I never enjoy anything more than being with you."

Mary felt her face going hot, and said nothing. She knew that she didn't quite deserve *that.*

He handed her a plate filled with little cucumber sandwiches that were slathered with cream cheese and dill and little pieces of watercress. They were delicious.

She took another sip of champagne.

"I missed you while you were gone," Seth told her, looking down at his glass. "I wondered what you were doing."

"Eating, mostly," Mary admitted, with a rueful smile.

"That, and visiting museums."

"You came back looking completely different," Seth told her. "You look like – like a *woman* now."

Mary glanced at him in amusement. "Like a sophisticated, *dangerous* woman?" she teased him.

He didn't meet her eyes, and looked suddenly downcast. "Don't laugh at me, Mary," he said quietly.

She put her glass down and reached for his hand. "I'm not laughing at you, Seth," she replied. "You're a sweet, thoughtful guy, and I – I –"

She tried to say it, but no sound came out.

Seth looked up at her. His eyes were a deep green, green as the forest behind him, and flecked with green light, like sunlight shining through spring leaves.

She found her voice.

"I – *like* you."

She would have said more, but Seth suddenly leaned over and kissed her. It was a soft, sweet kiss, tasting of cucumbers and wine.

To Mary's surprise, it felt kind of – *good*.

After their lips parted, Seth pulled back, and coughed, and busied himself with laying out the chicken salad, and pate, and grapes. He handed her a plate laden down with treats, and poured her another glass of wine.

Mary regarded him with some irony. Her sense of humor revived.

"You're not trying to get me *drunk*, are you, Seth?" she teased, and lifted the glass to her lips.

Seth shook his head, and passed her a plate of éclairs.

A little crooked smile tugged at Mary's lips. She put her wine glass down, and to her own surprise, she grabbed Seth's collar and pulled him to her mouth.

She wasn't entirely sure *how* to kiss him, but she figured that it was roughly like eating. So she nibbled on his lips as if they were éclairs – only, with more enthusiasm, and attention to detail.

She released him after a while, and leaned back to assess his face.

His eyes were closed, his brows were raised, and he was moving his mouth like a fish.

She twisted her mouth to one side, trying not to laugh. She was sure to regret this later. It was dumb to kiss Seth Troyer, it was against her better judgment, there was no future in it, and it was encouraging him when encouragement was the *last* thing he needed.

So she leaned in, and did it again.

CHAPTER SEVEN

Mary pulled back and glanced at Seth through her lashes. He reminded her of a line out of that book of French poetry --

Shot through the heart by Cupid's dart,

Captured, kiss'd, and slain.

Slain, that was it. Mary imagined Seth lying on the ground with a hand to his chest. She closed her eyes, and smirked, and released him.

Seth opened his eyes, went red to the roots of his hair, straightened his collar, and coughed. He went goofy and shy again, and suddenly had trouble meeting her eyes. But he had never had any trouble talking.

"Mary, what are you going to do now?" he asked. "You know – after – after all the –"

She leaned back against a tree trunk and ate an éclair. They had already polished off most of the champagne, and she was beginning to feel it. If she turned her head suddenly, the forest looked slightly off-kilter.

She shrugged and poured herself another glass of wine. "I don't know. I'm not going to be teaching at the school, that's for sure." She lifted the glass to her lips.

"You haven't made any plans?"

Mary shook her head and frowned. "No, not yet."

Seth looked down at the ground.

"You -- you're *leaving*, aren't you, Mary?" he asked suddenly. "You're going to the *English*. I can see it on your face."

Mary rolled her eyes to his in surprise.

"How –"

"Oh, I don't blame you," Seth added earnestly. "You just aren't cut out to be an Amish woman. Just like I'm not cut out to be an Amish man."

He looked up at her again. "Just don't leave without telling me – okay, Mary? Because if you leave, I want to come with you."

Mary stared at him in amazement. How had he known? And how had he managed to put her on the spot yet again?

But since Seth had somehow read her mind, she didn't see any reason to deny it.

"Yeah, I guess I'm leaving," she told him, "but not anytime soon. I can't leave *now*. I don't have a job, or any way to make money. I don't even know where I want to go, yet."

She gave him a direct look. "And you can't just *come with me* -- it wouldn't be proper."

Seth twisted a piece of grass between his fingers. "I know a place we can go, Mary. My oldest cousin went to the English ten years ago. I've been talking to her, off and on, for the last six months.

"She says that we can come and live with her, if we want to leave. Until we get jobs, at least, and maybe longer."

Mary looked up at him.

"*We?*"

Seth shrugged, and smiled. "Yeah. *I'm* leaving, and I thought I'd give you the option to join me -- just in case, you know, you might want to.

"And Becky's very nice, Mary. You'll like her, and you don't have to worry about things being awkward. Becky would give us different rooms."

"Where does she live?" Mary murmured. She tried to keep her voice casual, but her heart was thrumming. The chance to leave, to leave *right now*, was the last thing she'd expected Seth to offer her during a spring picnic, but -- as usual – he'd surprised her.

And thrilled her -- *and* scared her to death.

"Becky and her husband live in a little town in Delaware. They're about five minutes from the beach," Seth told her. "I've been there once; they have a nice big house. Lots of room."

Mary glanced up at him. "I don't know, Seth."

"Just think about it. But, Mary –" he reached out and took her hand "don't go unless you tell me first, okay? Or at least, don't go without telling me if you have somewhere to stay, when you go. Even if you don't decide to leave with me. I just want to be sure you're okay."

Mary looked at him ruefully. That freakish thing was happening to her eyes again. This time, Seth almost looked *hot*.

"Okay, Seth. I promise," she told him.

"Thank you, Mary. That takes a lot off my mind."

Mary stared at him, wondering what *other* secret plans Seth Troyer was hiding behind that innocent exterior. World domination, for all she knew. He was, apparently, a deep one.

"What are *you* going to do, once you leave, Seth?" she asked, tilting her head.

He shrugged. "Get my GED, and a driver's license. Find a

job, and a place. And then, I plan to work my way through college."

"That's right, the engineering thing," Mary murmured.

"Yeah. I won't be sitting on my hands," he assured her. "I have *big* plans."

Mary looked at him, and a slow smile crept over her lips. *I'll just bet you do*, she thought, and shook her head.

"I hope you're going to be a part of my future, Mary," he told her shyly.

Mary squirmed, and slid her hand out of his. "Just *leaving* is enough for me right now, Seth," she answered uncomfortably. "Maybe too much."

"I understand," he replied slowly, and his tone was a little crestfallen.

To Mary's surprise, the wounded sound in his voice gave her something almost like heartburn. She put a hand to her chest, frowning.

"It's getting late. I guess I better get you back home," Seth added, sighing. "Your parents will think I've kidnapped you."

Mary thought of her mother's excited face, and almost laughed out loud. But it would hardly be good manners to indulge her sense of irony in front of Seth.

They packed up the picnic basket with the leftovers, and

the bowls and dishes and glasses, and the empty wine bottle. Mary shook out the blanket and folded it up into a neat square.

Seth stowed the basket in the back seat and helped Mary up into the buggy. As he turned the horse around, and the buggy began to move down the forest road, Mary asked: "When do you plan to go, Seth?"

He gave her a sideways glance, and shrugged.

"You tell me, Mary. Because that depends on *you*."

CHAPTER EIGHT

A soft blue twilight had fallen over the house when Seth's buggy finally pulled up in front of their yard. The windows glowed yellow, and crickets hummed in the grass.

Mary clasped her hands in her lap. "T-thank you, Seth," she stammered, surprised by a sudden wave of shyness. "It's been a very nice –"

But Seth didn't let her finish. He leaned over and kissed her, this time boldly, and her eyebrows shot up.

When they parted, he said: "Just let me know. Do you still have your cell phone?"

She nodded.

"You can call me whenever you like."

Mary looked up at him in astonishment. "I will," she answered faintly.

She climbed out, but then twisted back to face him. "I may not decide right away, Seth," she warned. "You might not want to wait for me."

"I'll wait," he told her, and shook the reins.

The horse broke into a gentle canter, and Seth's buggy rounded the curve in the road and gradually faded into the deepening shadows.

But Mary stood watching long after it had disappeared from sight.

***

When Mary finally entered the house, both of her parents were sitting in the living room. They looked up as she entered.

"Where were you, Mary?" her father asked. "We were worried about you."

"Oh, Seth Troyer came by in his buggy and asked me to go for a ride with him," Mary answered, as nonchalantly as she could. "He took me on a picnic."

Her parents exchanged a significant look, and her mother only partially repressed a delighted smile.

"Oh! Well, *that's* all right, then," she murmured. "Seth is such a fine young man! I hope you were nice to him, Mary?"

Mary bit her lip, and felt a pang of guilt.

"I tried to be."

She looked at their unsuspecting faces, and her guilt deepened. She had dreamed of leaving for years, but now that it came right down to it -- how could she just *disappear* one day? It would devastate her parents, and she couldn't bear to think about that.

"I'm going up to bed," she told them, "…unless you need me for anything?"

"No, dear, you go on," her mother smiled. "Sweet dreams."

Mary climbed the stairs to her bedroom and closed the door behind her. She walked across the room and paused just in front of the window.

Outside, fireflies were rising from the fields by the hundreds. The cool twilight air was alive with stars. A little breath of air moved the curtain. It smelled fresh and sweet, like mown grass.

Mary sank down onto the floor and propped her elbows on the open sill. Seth's invitation danced before her eyes like one of the fireflies, twinkling seductively.

She had dreamed of this all her life, but she had hardly dared to hope that it would ever come true. A *month* ago she couldn't have imagined it.

But then she had flown to Paris, and the minute she'd

stepped off the plane, she knew she could never stay in this place.

Her parents' world was beautiful, it was safe, it was all she had ever known. But in Paris, she'd come to understand that they had been living on a tiny island – an island surrounded by a vast ocean.

And now Seth Troyer was inviting her to come with him, and sail off the edge of the map.

Mary imagined what would happen if she left. Her mouth twisted to one side. The children at the school might miss her, a little, but she knew that if Cora returned, they'd forget all about *her*.

She had no big circle of friends or string of boys to mourn her departure. No one her own age, aside from Cora, had more than tolerated her. There would be no painful partings there.

Cora was here, and *they* were friends, but now that Cora was busted, and didn't have a cell phone any more, she couldn't even call her to talk on the phone.

Mary sighed.

But then there was her mamm and daed. They were here, forever, and if she left, they would be crushed.

Water smeared and blurred the little firefly lights. It would be cruel for her parents, she knew. They would do anything in their power to keep her from leaving. For them, there was only one place for her – *here*.

All that was on one side.

But then, Mary imagined what would happen, if she *didn't* leave.

Seth was the only boy who had ever paid her any attention at all, and he was leaving.

If she stayed behind, she would continue to be Mary Stoltzfus, the odd, bookish Amish girl that no one wanted to sit with, and who couldn't get a man.

She would sit here at this window, looking out at this same meadow, every night of her life, dreaming of the world she had lost, and of the life she wanted, but couldn't live.

It would be like dying.

Mary swiped her eyes with her sleeve. She looked up silently at the sky, frowning.

This is not a rejection, she thought.

I still believe in You. I still want us to be okay.

I just don't belong here, that's all.

I hope You understand.

Her thoughts returned to her parents, chatting in the living room below. She might not have had the closest relationship to her parents, but she loved them, even if she didn't always say so, and she knew that they loved her.

She bowed her head.

Please help them when I go. Especially Mamm. She won't understand at all. Please help her to be okay.

And please – don't let them slam the door. Please talk them into letting me come back, now and then.

Amen.

Mary Stoltzfus sighed, and lowered her head onto her arms.

CHAPTER NINE

"No more crying."

Cora lifted her face, and Isaac gently blotted the last tear away.

When their own door had closed behind them at last, Cora twined her arms around Isaac's neck, anticipating a more intimate welcome than he had been able to show her in public.

But to her confusion, Isaac simply took her in his arms, closed his eyes, and *hugged* her.

Cora smiled, and waited for more, but *more* was not forthcoming.

She frowned, and smiled, and ran her fingers through his curling hair.

"Isaac, are you – are you hungry?" she asked.

He shook his head.

"Then -- *kiss* me."

But he didn't seem to be paying attention. He just stood there, with his arms around her, not moving, not doing anything, except that his lips moved slightly.

Almost like he was *praying*.

Cora frowned again.

"Isaac, is something wrong?" A lingering fear stabbed her. "You're not angry after all – *are you?*"

"No, no, no," Isaac mumbled, shaking his head. "I'm not angry."

"Then what *is* it? You were so friendly in the buggy. Don't stop now," she whispered, and kissed his ear gently. "Aren't you glad that I'm home?"

"*Very* glad," he murmured devoutly.

Cora smiled, and was confused, but unbuttoned his shirt and loosened it with her hands. She ran her fingers over his chest, and his shoulders.

"*How* I've missed the feel of your arms, Isaac," she sighed, closing her eyes. "I dreamed of them at night," she smiled.

But still Isaac said nothing, and did nothing. Cora's eyebrows twitched together.

"Isaac, something *is* wrong," she objected, pulling back from him. "Why won't you *kiss* me? Are you tired?"

Isaac nodded. "*Yes,* I'm tired, Cora," he stammered, and smiled apologetically. "I – I had to walk a long way last night."

Cora frowned in confusion. "You walked in the *dark?*" she objected. "Why, Isaac?"

Isaac stretched and yawned. "Oh, Cora, I'm sorry, I can hardly stay awake," he replied. "You'll have to ask me tomorrow. Now that you're back home, all I want to do is rest."

Cora's frown lifted. She stood on tiptoe and kissed his chin. "Poor Isaac, go to bed then," she soothed. "You deserve your rest."

But she watched him in puzzlement as he turned away, kicked off his shoes, and stumbled to the bedroom.

After he had gone, she put her hands on her hips in consternation.

It was a first.

Isaac had turned down an *invitation.*

Cora untied her apron, and folded it into a neat square. She stepped out of her shoes, and carefully unrolled her stockings, and rolled them back up again.

When she padded into their bedroom, it was dark. Isaac was already splayed out face down on the bed, fast asleep. The sound of gentle snoring rose from his pillow.

Cora stuck her lip out a little, and pulled her dress off a little harder than she had to.

She had been looking forward to a *much* different end to this evening.

But when she crawled into bed at last, the sound of Isaac's exhausted snoring melted her pique. It was impossible to listen to that sweet sound and stay cross. Poor Isaac – he worked *so* hard.

And it had been a very long, *trying* day.

She leaned over, and kissed his cheek gently, and then rolled over to find her own rest.

***

When Cora woke up the next morning, she turned her head to find that Isaac was gone. She frowned, and checked the clock.

It was five a.m.

She rose and pulled on a robe. The scent of frying bacon and the crackle of frying eggs drew her into the kitchen.

To her astonishment, Isaac was fully dressed, and making *breakfast*.

Cora smiled – and frowned.

"Why, Isaac, how *sweet*," she said, but her eyebrows asked a question. "You didn't have to do this. I'm always *happy* to make breakfast."

Isaac smiled at her. "I woke up early, so I just went ahead and did it," he shrugged.

Cora took a bite of buttered toast. "It *is* kind of nice to have someone else cook for a change," she admitted. "Thank you." She reached up and kissed him.

He smiled, and offered his cheek to be kissed, but made no move to kiss her back. Cora searched his face with her eyes, but his expression was quiet and calm.

She frowned.

"Sit down, Cora," he was saying, "I want to talk to you."

He dried his hands and sat down at the table opposite her. He looked over at her with serious eyes.

"I don't think our situation is going to get any better on its own," he said quietly. "The job at the Hauser's is *over*. There are no others right now. I need to do something to get money coming into this house, or we'll have to move."

Cora reached for his hand.

"Joseph said something to me yesterday. He suggested that I rent the lower half of this house, and use it to sell furniture.

He said that I should set up my own business. I'm really thinking about taking Joseph's advice. But I can't make that kind of decision without you. What do you think, Cora?"

Cora brightened. "Oh, Isaac, that's a wonderful idea!" she cried. "All your things are so beautiful, any business of yours is *sure* to be a success! And you know I'd do anything you need," she assured him warmly. "I'm not at the school anymore," she added more quietly, "so I have the time."

"Thank you, Cora," Isaac said softly. "That means a lot to me. But your brother made another suggestion, too," he went on. "One that I *didn't* like so much. He offered to loan us the money."

Cora repressed a sigh.

"I know you don't like to borrow money from anybody, Isaac," she said softly, "but honestly, Joes wouldn't offer if he didn't *want* to, and if he didn't *believe* in you."

Isaac shook his head. "Joseph is good to offer, but I hate it, Cora. I'm only doing it because there's no other way. But I want you to know this -- he's loaning it to us at the going rate. No special family deal. It's just like we were going to the bank."

Cora reached out and caressed his cheek. "I *know*, Isaac," she smiled. "And not because it's Joes. I know because it's *you*."

CHAPTER TEN

The next day Isaac came back from Gideon Miller's with the keys to the first floor of the house. He lifted them in the air and smiled at Cora.

"Ready to go see?"

She held out her hand, and he took it.

There was a little locked door at the end of the upstairs hall. Cora watched as Isaac opened it up. Ever since they moved there, she had wondered what was on the other side.

The door swung back to reveal a narrow staircase that ran down into darkness.

Isaac led her down the steps to another door, which he also had to unlock. That door opened into a small, dark room.

Cora swung a flashlight beam around the room in a wide arc. The little room looked as if it had been abandoned for a long time. There was one dusty card table, and scattered paper litter over the floor.

Isaac led her through a door to the left, and they entered a huge, dark room, the main room on the first floor. Office furniture and lumber filled it, and moving through the space was like navigating a maze.

It was broad daylight outside, but the front windows were so dirty that only a dull brown light seeped in.

"It's worse than I thought," Isaac marveled. "The Millers must not have used this place for *years*."

"How are we ever going to get all this junk out of here, Isaac?" Cora wailed softly. "It'll take *weeks*!"

Isaac scanned the distant corners of the room – all of them stacked to the ceiling with lumber and furniture.

"We'll just have to do the best we can, Cora," Isaac answered softly, but his expression was less sure than his words.

Cora set her mouth. "Well, I can start by washing those windows," she sighed, "so at least we can have some *light* in here. I'll bring down some of those camping lanterns. And the mop."

Isaac looked at her fondly, and rolled up his sleeves. "If I can get to the back door, and open it then I can start taking out some of this lumber."

Their eyes met in the gloom, and Isaac cracked a wide,

rueful smile.

"We're both going to end up looking like we've been dragged through the mud," Cora giggled.

"You'd be beautiful even then," he told her.

Cora laughed, wiggled her hips, and smiled back at Isaac over her shoulder. He whistled ruefully.

But to her disappointment, he *still* disappeared into the maze of lumber, leaving her to wash windows.

***

Two days later, the windows in the lower floor were sparkling clean and no less than half a dozen lanterns gave off little pools of light. Cora had mopped and dusted the little room at the foot of the stairs until there wasn't a grain of dirt left, and Isaac had carved out several paths through the storage room: one from the little office room, one to the back door, one to the front door, and two more leading to a bathroom and another small room on the other side of the house.

It was nearing dinnertime, and they had both worked all day. Cora swiped her brow with her elbow, because she was wearing filthy gloves and didn't want to make herself any dirtier than she already was.

"I'm going to go fix dinner, Isaac," she called.

A grunt from somewhere on the other side of the room signaled that Isaac had heard, even if she couldn't see him. There was suddenly a tremendous clatter, like an avalanche.

"Isaac, are you all right?" she called.

"Yeah. A bunch of shelves fell off the top of this" – there was more clattering – "*bookcase*."

"Be careful," Cora called after him.

***

When she got to the top of the stairs and stepped out into their clean, bright apartment, Cora sighed in relief, stripped off her filthy clothes, and walked naked to the bathroom. She couldn't *think* about handling food until she had scrubbed her skin and her hair. She felt as if she was *coated* in dust.

She turned on the water, sat on the edge of the tub and soaping up her washcloth, lathered up, scrubbing the grime from her skin as the tub filled. When it was full enough for a bath, she sat inside and let it rinse the soap from her skin. Then, she lathered up her hair and scrubbed her scalp hard; ducking beneath the water a couple of times to clean her hair.

When she finally stepped out again, she felt squeaky-clean, and fresh as a newborn.

She shrugged into a robe and put her hair up in a towel.

When she came back out into the hall, Isaac appeared at

the top of the staircase. His whole face was brown with dust, and his blue eyes were startling in contrast.

Cora put a hand over her mouth. "Oh, Isaac, you're filthy – you look like you just crawled out of a *mine*!" she giggled.

"I *feel* like a miner, too," he groaned, and would have gone into the bedroom, but Cora shrieked and waved her hands.

"Isaac, *please* take off those filthy things and go get a tub!" she cried. "I'll have to mop the floor if you track across it in those shoes!"

He kicked off his huge shoes, groaned, and stumbled into the bathroom. The sound of running water soon followed.

Cora picked his clothes up with two fingers, carried them to the washroom, and dumped them in the dirty clothes bin.

She looked into the kitchen, and at the empty skillet sitting on the stove, and sighed.

Then she looked back toward the bathroom, and a slow smile dawned across her face.

She walked into the steamy bathroom, and Isaac was just getting out of the shower. He looked up as she entered, and reached for a towel.

She leaned against the doorway, and paused to enjoy the sight of her strapping husband. His bare back was turned toward her momentarily. It was a view she usually enjoyed, but this time, what she saw made her brows rush together.

"Isaac, *what happened to your back*? Those shelves must have scraped you when they fell!"

He half-turned his head. His eyes looked startled.

"My back?"

"Your back has red marks all over it!" she exclaimed, and would have gone to inspect them closer, but Isaac quickly pulled on his robe. He stood there for a few moments, facing away from her, not moving, not saying anything.

Then he turned. His eyes had a strange look. They were grim, but they also held – something like dread.

"Come and sit down, Cora," he said quietly. "I have something to tell you."

CHAPTER ELEVEN

He took her hand and led her into the living room, and sat down beside her on the sofa.

Cora looked at him sadly. She had the sense that something bad was coming.

"Isaac, it's been *days* since I came back," she said softly, "and you haven't touched me once. I know that *something* is wrong."

She looked up into his eyes, searching them. "Is it – is it about what I did, Isaac? The – the pills? Because I want you to understand, *I want a baby*, too –"

Isaac looked down, and his cheeks flushed a dull red.

"No, Cora, it's not that. I was wrong about that. I'm sorry."

Confusion roiled her thoughts.

"Then *what's wrong*?"

He looked up, and his eyes were full of pity, as if he hurt for her. He tried to say something, and couldn't.

"You don't have to be worried, Isaac," she assured him. "Whatever it is, I could *never* be angry with you, and I had no right to be, anyway. You were right, and I was wrong."

Isaac looked down again. A tiny muscle twitched in his jaw.

"Cora, the thing I'm *most* sorry about is that I didn't listen to you. I could have saved us both a lot of heartache, if I had."

Cora watched him with a puzzled frown.

Isaac took a deep breath and continued: "You asked me not to take that job at Levi Hauser's, because – because Leah was there."

Comprehension began to dawn over Cora's face. She frowned, and Isaac grabbed her hands in his and held them firmly. He looked into her eyes.

"I didn't finish out the job at the Hauser's, Cora. I came home early. In the dark. *Because--*"

Cora's bright eyes caught fire. "Leah Hauser tried to *seduce* you!" she cried. "That's what you're trying to tell me -- *isn't it*, Isaac?"

Isaac looked down.

"Yes."

"Oh!" An inarticulate scream clawed up from Cora's throat, and she thrashed against his hands. "Let me *go,* Isaac!"

Isaac blinked back tears and held her. "Nothing *happened,* Cora," he added quickly, "I didn't *let* anything happen."

"I'll *kill* her!" Cora shrieked, and fought against his hands. "I told her what I'd do if she *ever* put her hands on you again –"

"Cora, I didn't *let* anything happen. *I sent her away.* We didn't – we *never –*"

"Let me *go,* Isaac!" she shrieked. "Take your hands *off* me!"

"Cora –"

"Let me go!"

He released her, and she thrashed away so violently that her hair burst free and spilled wildly through the air.

Then she clambered up and made for the bedroom.

Isaac watched her with dark, worried eyes. "What are you doing, Cora?"

"I'm going to get dressed."

"Why?"

"Why do you *think?*" she cried.

Isaac stood and put his hands up in a gesture of truce.

"Cora, you can't go to the Hauser's. And there's no *need* to go."

"No *need*?" Cora cried. "If she had only stolen my *bag*, or my *money*, I could've forgiven it! But to steal my *husband!*" Cora's mouth clamped to a straight, angry line. "She may as well have *stabbed* me!"

Isaac rose. "Cora, *think*. You're already in trouble. If you pick a fight with Leah Hauser now, you might be shunned!"

"Don't try to stop me, Isaac," she warned him.

"Cora, I can't let you do this, you'll be ruined –"

"You can't lock me in, Isaac!"

Isaac reached out and took her shoulders. "Cora, calm down. I tell you, *nothing* happened."

Cora struggled angrily against his grip. "You told me yourself that she tried to seduce you, and the evidence is on your back! You call that *nothing*?" She pushed against him as hard as she could, but Isaac's chest was like a tree trunk.

"Cora, stop fighting me," Isaac urged her. "Calm down and behave like a civilized woman!"

"So now I'm uncivilized! Is that what she told you, Isaac?" she demanded. *"What did she do to you?"*

Isaac grappled with her hands, frowning. "Cora, if you don't calm down, I'm going to –"

Cora pulled back suddenly and glared at him. "What, Isaac? *What* are you going to do? Are you going to lock me in, like a *prisoner*? Why are you stopping me? Are you afraid I'm going to *hurt Leah*?"

Isaac pinched his lips into an exasperated line. "I don't care about Leah Hauser at all. But I care about *you,* and you're about to do something that could –"

Cora didn't wait for him to finish. She turned suddenly and dashed into the bedroom. Isaac watched in amazement then bounded after her just in time to prevent her from slamming the door. When he threw it open, she was standing at the open window, eyeing the tool shed a few feet below. His mouth dropped open.

"Cora, what are you *doing?*"

She grabbed the sill, preparing to climb out, and he reached out just in time to tear her from the brink.

She catapulted into his arms, and the momentum sent him crashing back onto the bed. She twisted like a cat, and would have jumped up again, but he held her fast.

"Let me go!" she shrieked.

"No."

She screamed, curled her hands into fists, and beat on his chest as hard as she could. But Isaac merely lay quiet, and held her.

Slowly her fists slowed, and grew weaker, and uncurled.

After a long while, Cora stopped, and squeezed her eyes shut. She lay panting on his chest.

Then she leaned her head wearily against him.

"I'm sorry that I had to tell you," Isaac said quietly. "But I couldn't let it stay a secret between us. The guilt was eating me alive."

"*Nothing happened*, Isaac?"

"She threw herself at me, just like she always does," he replied patiently. "But *I didn't sleep with her*, Cora."

She raised her eyes to his, and he held her gaze.

"You've never lied to me, Isaac. I believe you. *But I can't stand to think of her hands on you!*"

Isaac looked down at her sadly, took one of her hands, and placed it over his heart. "It doesn't matter what she did," he told her. "You're the only one who's ever touched me *here*."

A tear trickled down Cora's cheek, but a faint smile also dawned across her face.

"Will you – will you let me touch you there *again*, Isaac?" she whispered.

He looked at her sadly, and for answer, devoured the question off her upturned lips.

CHAPTER TWELVE

The next morning, the sound of a warbling bird wafted sweetly through the open bedroom window and woke Isaac. The morning air made the bedroom cool, and fresh, and fragrant of new leaves.

Isaac opened his eyes. Mottled, green-gold oak leaves filled the view outside the window. The sky just beyond was blue and cloudless.

He had overslept.

He stretched his arms out, and smiled, and rolled over to reach for Cora, but the bed beside him was empty. At first he saw nothing wrong with this.

Then his eyes widened. He threw the sheets off.

"Cora?"

***

Cora opened the door of the little town grocery and picked up a basket. She browsed through the produce section, picking out Isaac's favorites, and to all appearances was as calm as dawn.

But she was *burning up* on the inside.

Isaac had done everything in his power to soothe her. He had comforted her all night with his words and his body.

But the fiery anger was still there, boiling very close to the surface.

Cora met the eyes of a passing shopper, and smiled dryly, thinking that the woman would've been shocked to know what the prim Amish housewife was *really* thinking.

The woman's eyes moved down from Cora's face and rested briefly on her hands.

Cora looked down. Her fingers had gouged five little holes into a tomato. She placed it quickly into her basket.

A good Amish person shouldn't be having such violent thoughts, she knew. It was wrong to harbor them, wrong to linger over them.

But in spite of what she should feel, the only thing she wanted, and *very badly* too, was to catch Leah Hauser in some lonely spot and thrash her within an inch of her life.

At the moment at least, the fantasy didn't give her a speck of guilt – just a grim satisfaction. And in spite of Isaac's warnings, she couldn't stop imagining it.

Isaac was worried about what would happen later, but Isaac couldn't possibly understand how she felt.

Isaac had never had a rival who was willing to do *anything*.

Cora picked up a head of lettuce and dropped it into the basket with a *thud.*

She didn't let herself dwell on what she would do the next time she saw Leah Hauser. She couldn't go there.

A big, hard lump formed in her throat. It felt unfair that *she* was the one in trouble with the elders. What were English clothes, and cell phones, when Leah Hauser had just tried to *steal her husband*?

Cora threw a stalk of bruised celery back into the bin.

But life wasn't fair, because *she* was going to have to repent, and Leah Hauser was going to get away scot-free, because no one but Isaac knew about her crimes, and Isaac would never make serious trouble for someone else – even *Leah Hauser*.

Her sense of injustice welled up suddenly into an angry prayer:

Oh God, why did this happen? Weren't You the one who gave Isaac to me? Are You going to let Leah Hauser get away with trying to steal him?

She clenched her fist.

Oh God – expose her crimes!

Cora bowed her head, but resentment was like a wall all around her, and she had no sense of any reply.

She sighed, thinking that she could probably save her breath. God was probably angry with her for her vengeful thoughts.

She chose a few more items and joined the line at the checkout, where she stood listlessly gazing at the register.

Elie Meissen was busy gossiping with a man at the counter. Cora lifted her eyes in boredom and scanned the street outside through the store window. The occasional buggy rolled past as people began to arrive in town for their mid-morning shopping.

As she watched, a strangely familiar vehicle rolled past outside. Cora stiffened. It was – yes, it was -- *Levi Hauser's buggy!*

Cora stiffened. Her heart jumped into her throat.

Then she pulled her lips down.

Elie Meissen suddenly stopped talking and turned toward the door in confusion.

"Cora! *Cora Muller!*"

The little shopping basket was lying on the ground, and the

vegetables were rolling here and there on the floor.

***

Cora dashed outside and turned to watch as the buggy rolled down the street. It was a good two blocks ahead of her, and going at a fast clip, but she was determined to catch it.

Cora dodged around other pedestrians, not caring what they thought. She crashed into an old man outside the candy shop and almost knocked him down.

"Oh – I'm sorry, I'm sorry," she murmured, but didn't stop.

When she turned back, the buggy had pulled almost out of sight. She cursed under her breath, and gathered her skirts to *run*.

A sudden dark flash on her right was the only warning she had before the world turned upside down. Cora sprawled into space and fell full-length on the ground.

"*Oh!*" She screamed in frustration, and turned her head to see what had taken her down.

To her astonishment, it was *Mary Stoltzfus*.

"Oh – hi, Cora," she drawled, arms folded. "Sorry about that."

Cora's face gathered into a knot. She beat the ground with her fist.

"You *tripped* me!" she cried.

"You were clumsy," Mary amended. She put out a hand, and pulled Cora up.

Cora dusted her dress off, and looked at Mary with a kindling eye. "What are you even doing in town, Mary Stoltzfus!" she complained.

"Shopping," Mary replied calmly. "What were you doing?"

Cora looked up, searching for the buggy, but it was gone.

"You know, I was hoping I might run into you," Mary told her, and responded to Cora's frown with, "*Sorry*. But I really *did* want to catch up with you. We haven't had a chance to talk since – well, you know. I wanted to say thanks for sticking up for me with the school board. You didn't have to. It was nice of you."

Cora shrugged, and licked a scrape on her thumb.

"Why don't we have lunch. My treat." Cora hesitated, and Mary added: "Unless you're scared to be seen in town with a *rebel* like me?"

Cora sputtered out a grudging laugh. "Oh, all right, Mary," she laughed. "You know I can't stay mad at *you*."

But she turned and looked back over her shoulder more than once, as they walked away

CHAPTER THIRTEEN

"So, are you going to tell me what *that* was all about, or do I get to make up a rumor?" Mary asked, as she unfolded a menu at the little café. "Either way works for me."

Cora glared at her.

"You tripped me *deliberately*!" she cried.

"I just know what happens when you and Leah Hauser get too close together," Mary replied, flipping the menu. "Oh – the dessert looks good today. New York cheesecake."

Cora turned unhappy eyes to the street outside their booth. "I can't tell you, Mary," she said quietly. "Some things are too personal to share, even with your best –"

She broke off and went red.

"That's all right," Mary replied calmly. "It's not hard to

figure out. There's only *one* thing I've ever seen you go postal over."

Cora frowned.

"Mary, I can't tell *anyone*," she pleaded. "It's a *private* thing."

Mary raised her eyebrows, and continued to scan the menu. "It wasn't very private just *now*," she said. "Everybody on the street was watching you."

Cora shifted uncomfortably in her seat.

"Knocking the old man down was a nice touch. It made you look *good* and crazy."

"I didn't mean to do that."

Mary lowered her menu and looked at Cora sympathetically. "Look, I know it's none of my business. But you *do* know you can't attack Leah Hauser in the middle of Main Street – *right*?" Cora scowled, and Mary put the menu up again. "Oooo-*kay*."

Cora looked around her, and then down at her lap, and the over at Mary.

"Mary, if I tell you, will you *swear* not to tell anyone else? Not even your parents?" she whispered.

Mary met her eyes and nodded. "I promise."

Cora looked down again and sighed. "Isaac was laid off at

his job," she whispered. "He found some work at Levi Hauser's, but he had to stay out at the Hauser farm for a week. While he was there" – she ground her teeth – "Leah Hauser tried to *seduce* him!"

Mary's eyes widened. She whistled soundlessly.

"Wow. *That* would do it, all right," she marveled. "You know, I should lecture you, Cora, but I can't. I would've done *just the same*, in your shoes."

"I can't help it. I want to *kill* her!" Cora hissed.

The waitress bustled up and smiled brightly. "What can I get you ladies today?" she chirped.

"Give us a minute."

As soon as she was gone, Cora added softly: "Isaac didn't *let* Leah seduce him, but it makes me crazy to think that she *tried*!"

"So what are you going to do?"

Cora gnawed a nail. "I don't know. I don't *trust* myself."

"You're going to have to face her sooner or later. And you've joined the church now. You can't just go for her throat! If I were you, I'd play it cool," Mary urged. "*Very* cool. Pretend you don't know about it. Isaac told her to get lost, right? So maybe she'll give up and go hunting for somebody else."

"She'd *better*," Cora muttered. "But she probably *won't*."

"It sounds like a crime of opportunity to me," Mary muttered. "It happened because he was right under her nose, but she won't have a chance to get that close to him a second time. So you can *afford* to play it cool," Mary whispered. "Anyway, the fact that Isaac *told* you about it proves that you don't have anything to worry about. That's what *matters*, right?"

Cora blinked and smiled at her friend. She nodded, and looked down. "Thank you, Mary," she said quietly. "You make me feel better. It feels good to talk to somebody about it. I've been *burning up* inside."

"*Hmm*. Leah is the one who should be burning," Mary shrugged, lifting a glass of tea to her lips. "She made a play for Isaac, and it blew up on her. She *lost*."

Cora nodded. "I think that's why she hates me," she said thoughtfully. "This whole thing between me and Leah started out to be about Isaac. For me, that's all it was *ever* about. But for Leah, I'm not sure it's all about Isaac anymore, or at least, not *just* about him. It's bigger than that.

"Because I got the boy that Leah wanted. I fought her for him, and I won *then*, too. She tried to turn all my old friends against me, but they stopped listening to her. She used her mother to try to keep me from getting the job at the school, but I got the job anyway.

"I think now, she just wants to *prove* something. Like she's *better* than me. Or, if she can't do *that*, still make things as miserable for me, as she can."

"So don't let her."

Cora picked at the tablecloth. "I don't know if I can play it cool, Mary. If I lost Isaac, I'd just -- *die*."

Mary pulled her mouth to one side and glanced out the window. Finally she said, "Leah is going to yank your chain if you let her, Cora. You *have* to control yourself."

"I know."

"Because your butt is *still* on the griddle about the cell phone thing," Mary sighed. "I hope you repent really well, because you need to be *convincing*!"

Mary looked down at her hands and sighed. "I never thanked you for that, by the way. I know you only used the cell phone to get me to give Seth a chance. It was really nice of you, Cora. I appreciate it."

Cora looked up sharply. Delight flashed in her eyes. "Mary Stoltzfus, are you *going out with Seth?*" she cried.

Mary smiled slowly. "Yeah. I am. And you were right. He's a really nice guy. A handsome guy."

"I'm so glad for you, Mary! And I *knew* you'd see it!" Cora nodded. "Seth is a little hunk."

Mary looked at her friend fondly. "You've done a lot for me. I owe you, Cora."

Cora shrugged, and went pink. "You don't owe me, Mary. I would've gotten into trouble sooner or later *anyway*."

"You're probably right," Mary agreed wryly, "but I hate to think that you might *really* crash and burn one day. Try to stay on the straight and narrow, will you?

"Because I might not be standing there, the next time you want to do something crazy."

CHAPTER FOURTEEN

After their lunch, Mary and Cora lingered on the sidewalk outside the café, and Cora reached over impulsively and hugged her friend.

"I'm *so* glad I ran into you today, Mary. You know what I mean!" she laughed, rubbing her elbow. "Tell Seth I said hi," she added mischievously.

"I will," Mary said quietly. "I'll see you around, Cora. *Remember what I said.*"

"Why don't you and Seth come visit us?" Cora smiled.

"Yeah, we'll – we'll have to do that."

Cora waved over her shoulder, and hurried down the street.

Mary watched her go wistfully, remembering all the things they had been through together. Then she shook her head, and turned in the opposite direction.

***

Mary had come to town to say her goodbyes to Cora, and to the neighborhood. She had meant to take a leisurely stroll through town, a kind of farewell tour, but the stares she was getting made her change her plans. To be fair, some of her neighbors might not have been expressing disapproval: she looked about as un-Amish as it was possible to look, with her short crop of jet-black hair, her painted lips, and her English clothes.

Some of them might not have *recognized* her.

Mary walked about a block outside of town, and then cut across the fields, making her way home across country. It was a route she knew well, a well-worn maze of footpaths that countless children had beaten through the woods and pastures. High white clouds billowed in the sky above tilled brown fields. Here and there in the distance, men driving teams of horses planted grain. It was part of the familiar cycle she had seen played out over and over: tilling, planting, cultivating, reaping.

She skirted Enoch Horst's field, cutting through the little stand of trees along the creek, and along the path at the water's edge. It brought her to the schoolyard the back way, up from the far edge of the playground.

School was out, and the yard was empty.

Mary walked slowly through the schoolyard, past the

deserted softball diamond, the volleyball court, and the benches where she had spent so many hours.

She walked up to the back entrance, pulled a key out of her pocket, and opened the door.

The schoolroom was spotless and empty. The desks were set in neat rows, waiting patiently for the children to come crowding back in.

Mary swiped her fingertips across the blackboard, leaving four dark, soft marks across the surface.

She walked over to the little desk she had used as a teacher. Her old books were just where she had left them.

She looked up, and sighed, and pulled her wrist across her nose. Then she lifted the key by its little chain, and placed it reverently on the desk.

Then she walked out, closed the door behind her, and vanished into the woods beyond without a backward glance.

***

"*Mary*, there you are at last! Where have you *been* all day, girl?"

The sun was setting when Mary climbed the porch steps to her parents' house. Her mother was standing in the open door, and chided gently: "Give me a hand with the dishes. Dinner is already late."

Mary helped her mother silently, not trusting herself to speak. She hated to cry, and had held out all day but now she was perilously close to tears. She kept her head down, and her eyes averted, hoping that no one would notice.

Once the table had been laid out with plates and dishes and glasses and cups, stuffed cabbage, buttered corn, peas, and her mother's famous beef pot pie, they sat down at the table, as they always had.

Mary ate silently as her parents talked. She ate slowly, taking her time over each morsel.

"Mary, you haven't said much this evening," her father noticed.

Mary kept her eyes on her plate. She shrugged.

"Oh, she's probably thinking of a certain *young man*," her mother smiled. "Let her alone, Amos."

Mary swallowed hard. The last bite had stuck in her throat.

"Well, you're too young to get serious about any boy," her father told her. "And no respectable boy is going to ask, anyway, Mary, *unless* you join the church."

"Amos," Fannie said softly.

He coughed, and went back to eating.

Mary looked up suddenly. "It's all right, Daed," she murmured. "I know that you and Mamm just -- want the best for me."

Both of them stared at her, as if they couldn't believe their ears. Fannie looked at her husband, and they both went back to eating without comment.

After dinner, Mary cleared the table and volunteered to do the dishes. She stood at the sink, with her hands in hot, sudsy water, and listened to the sound of her parents talking in the living room, as they often did during the evening.

When she was finished, she walked softly up the stairs, and paused at the top momentarily.

Then she went inside her bedroom and closed the door quietly.

***

The moon was high in the sky outside her window, and the house was silent, when Mary saw the light flash in the yard below. It bloomed once, and was gone.

She turned and picked up her suitcase. It held the few things she was willing to carry away with her: her English clothes, her old journals, her cell phone, her Bible – and the book of French poetry that Seth had given her.

She paused in the doorway and looked back at her room: the simple little bed, the hooks for her clothes, the chest that had held her childhood toys.

Then she walked silently down the hall to her parent's bedroom door. She propped an envelope on the floor just outside, and then glided soundlessly down the stairs.

Seth was waiting for her on the porch.

"Ready?" he whispered.

She nodded, and led him out through the garden and across their fields to the road.

The distance seemed twice as far in the dark. Once something big and black jumped right in front of them, and Mary stifled a shriek. When Seth snapped the flashlight on, a startled deer stared at them for a split-second before bounding away.

Mary looked back over her shoulder at the house. It was still dark, still sleeping. The moon painted the roof silver, and cast shadows under the big trees.

"We shouldn't turn the light on again," Seth whispered. "Take my hand; I'll make sure you don't fall."

She held it out, and Seth grasped it, leading her through the bushes at the end of their fields. He helped her climb over the fence in the dark, and they stumbled down an embankment and onto the road.

"They're waiting for us a few miles away," Seth told her. "They can't come in too far, or they might be seen. Up for a stroll?"

"I'm game," Mary murmured. The cool night air was crisp and bracing, and her sense of adventure had revived.

It helped to leaven her sadness, her sense of loss.

They walked in silence for close to an hour. Even in the dark, Mary knew that they were approaching the county line.

Seth suddenly stopped and squeezed her hand reassuringly. "Look, Mary -- there they are."

He snapped the flashlight again, and down on the road ahead, a pair of headlights glowed in reply.

They picked up their pace. The car's engine hummed to life. A shiny black sedan soon met them in the road, and the passenger door swung open. The interior light flicked on, giving Mary a glimpse of a young, attractive couple. The woman leaned out and reached for Seth.

"I'm glad you came, Seth," she murmured, hugging him. "And this must be Mary?"

"This is my cousin, Becky Thompson," Seth explained.

"Hi," Mary said shyly, but there wasn't much time for introductions.

"Throw your bags on the seat and jump in," Becky told them.

Seth tossed their bags into the back seat, jumped in, and reached for her. Mary slid in beside him, and he put his arm around her.

The man at the wheel turned around in the road, shifted gears, and the engine revved. The car hurtled off through the darkness, leaving the moonlit fields, and Mary's childhood home, far behind.

She looked back through the rear window, but the dirt road behind them soon faded into darkness, and was gone.

CHAPTER FIFTEEN

They drove all night and the gentle motion of the car, and the monotonous hum of the engine, soon sent Mary to sleep on Seth's chest.

Her dreams were fitful and troubled. She was writing the letter again, trying to find the perfect words that would explain what she felt, and that wouldn't hurt her parents, but she finally had to admit defeat.

In the end, she had simply written:

Dear Mamm and Daed,

I love you, you're the best parents I could ever have had. You've always been there for me, and that's why it's so hard to write this letter.

As much as I love you, I can't stay here and be Amish. It's a good life for the ones who want it, but I need something different. I hope you understand.

I hope you'll let me come back sometime. I'd like to see you again. I hope that one day you'll be okay with that.

All my love,

Mary

P.S. Seth wanted to come with me. Please tell his parents that I won't let anything happen to him. I'll write to let you know how we're doing.

The letter faded as she drifted in and out of a restless twilight sleep. The sound of a car door opening, and a tiny, repetitive chime intruded on her dream. She turned her head, murmured, and fell back to sleep.

After a while, a bright light overhead made her frown and shield her eyes. A powerful scent filled the car.

A woman's voice floated into her dream. "We're almost there. We're just stopping to get some gas," it was saying, and she heard Seth's voice in reply, but the meaning of his words floated away.

She saw her father again, his serious brown eyes, and her mother smiling. Their faces bobbed through her dreams, mixing in with the school children, and the Louvre, and paintings of lace and voluptuous pearls. Cora's voice piped up suddenly, floating in the air like a bird's.

Someone was shaking her gently.

"*Look*, Mary," Seth urged.

She opened her eyes and squinted against the light. A pale pink morning had unfurled across the sky. Birds were wheeling all around the car, crying almost like children.

"It's the *ocean*," Seth smiled.

Mary sat up.

They were speeding along a flat, narrow road, and the land had fallen away all the way to the horizon. Off to the left, as far as the eye could see, was the ocean. Smooth, calm morning waves rippled gently to the white shore. The scent of salt water filled the air.

Mary had seen the ocean on her plane flight, but it had looked far away and unreal, like a big blue canvas.

But here, at ground level, it was like some huge animal. It was half asleep, in the pale pink morning, but it was always moving, murmuring to itself.

She turned to Seth, her eyes full of wonder. He grinned and squeezed her arm.

Becky put her elbow on the seat and turned back to look at them. "Good morning," she smiled. "I guess you two are getting hungry, huh?"

Neither of them spoke – it would have been rude to agree – but Becky just laughed. "We'll stop and grab something at the drive thru, and then we'll go home and crash."

Mary raised her brows, because she knew only one

meaning for *crash*; but Seth smiled at his cousin gratefully.

"We can't thank you enough," he said quietly.

"We're glad to do it, Seth," Becky assured him.

The car pulled into a fast-food drive thru, and the scent of coffee and hash browns reminded Mary that she was hungry. It was six a.m. by the sky, but at home, breakfast would have been long over by now.

Becky passed a paper bag back to them, and Seth reached into it and gave Mary a small sandwich with a sausage patty and an egg and a piece of cheese, and then a small packet of hash browns.

Mary and Seth exchanged a wordless glance. They were in no position to complain, and would never have done so anyway, but by Amish standards, a small sandwich and a handful of hash browns hardly qualified as a snack, let alone a breakfast.

But they thanked Becky and her husband, and ate silently.

The sedan re-entered the stream of traffic and made several turns off the main drag, and through various twisting byways to a quiet neighborhood with oak-shaded lanes and old, colonial houses.

Mary watched the prim rows of neat, English houses as they passed, each one with a shiny car in the driveway, and sometimes two. Loud music blared from one home as a teenager, about Seth's age, jumped into his car and turned the ignition.

They made one last turn, and rolled slowly down a quiet, dead-end street. The car finally pulled into the driveway of a two-story brick Tudor with clipped hedges and a massive oak tree in the front yard. A big Labrador retriever bounded out suddenly and jumped on the driver's side door.

"There's my big boy!" Becky said indulgently. "Have you missed us, Captain?"

The dog barked and wagged its tail furiously.

Mary looked up at the house. It was clean, and tidy, and attractive. For some reason, the presence of the dog reassured her. She didn't know why.

Seth turned to her and smiled. "We're here, Mary. You're going to *love* it, wait and see!"

Mary returned his smile, but in spite of the encouraging signs, and Seth's reassurance, she had never felt smaller, or *less* brave, in her life. She squinted up at the fancy English house.

She had known that this was going to be tough – but it had been less frightening for her to fly alone to *Paris*, than to take a ride with Seth Troyer to Delaware.

She picked up her suitcase and followed the others across the lawn and into the house. The interior was richly furnished with polished wooden floors, timbered ceilings, and real paintings on the wall, mostly of ships and the ocean. There was a big grandfather clock in the foyer, and lots of simple wooden furniture that looked Amish-made.

Seth's cousin had been raised Amish, of course.

Becky's husband put an arm around Seth's shoulders and led him upstairs. Becky waited for her in the hall.

"Let me show you to your room, Mary," she said.

They climbed the stairs and Becky showed Mary into a small paneled study with a fireplace and leaded windows facing the front yard and the left side of the house. There was a small sofa in brown toile on the far side of the room.

"The sofa makes out into a bed," Becky explained. "This will be your room while you're here. You just put your hands under the bottom edge of the sofa and pull it out. The door locks when you push this button" – she demonstrated -- "and there are sheets and a pillow in the chest."

Mary studied Becky Thompson. She was an attractive young woman who looked to be in her mid-thirties. Becky had short, sandy brown hair, and nice eyes that reminded her of Seth's, except that they were a plain hazel, instead of a vivid green.

"We're glad that you're here, Mary," Becky said kindly. "I know this has to be overwhelming for you, so take your time getting used to things. You're welcome to come down and join us anytime, but you don't have to, if you don't feel like it. We'll be eating lunch at noon."

"Thank you for everything," Mary said, in a small voice.

Becky only smiled, and closed the door behind her.

Mary walked to the sofa and sat down on it gingerly. She placed her suitcase on the polished floor. The room felt opulent, over-furnished, *strange*. There was a desk on the other side of the room, and a small, dead laptop sitting on it.

Mary stretched out on the sofa and rested her head on one of the pillows. She tried not to imagine what was happening back home at this moment, but it was impossible to block out the images that flooded her brain.

She saw her mother open their bedroom door, and find the note. She saw her face cloud, saw her hand go to her mouth. She saw her rush to her old bedroom, to find it empty.

Her father would have come to the door minutes later, pulling his suspenders over his shoulders. They were probably out searching for her now.

She knew they were going *crazy*.

She had managed to hold it all in thus far, but the dam finally broke. Mary's mouth twisted. She grabbed the pillow, jammed it over her face, and used it to muffle the sound of her grief.

CHAPTER SIXTEEN

Isaac had just mopped the last bit of gravy off of his breakfast plate, and Cora had just taken the dish from him, when there was a brisk knock at the door.

Cora raised her eyebrows. "Are you expecting anyone this early?" she asked, and Isaac shook his head.

He stood up and went to the door. When he opened it, their deacon and minister stood on the little landing.

"Good morning, Brother Muller."

Isaac went red to the roots of his hair. "Good morning brothers," he replied, and extended a hand. "Come in."

Deacon King and Minister Fisher took off their hats and entered. Isaac motioned toward the sofa, and shot a look at Cora. She was standing in the kitchen with her hands clasped together. Her face was as white as a sheet.

The men sat down on the sofa. Isaac sat in a chair facing

them, and motioned for Cora to join him. She moved quickly to his side.

"Brother Muller, we're here at the request of the bishop," said Minister Fisher.

"How is he doing?" Isaac asked quickly, and they shook their heads.

"He's well," said Deacon King. "He wasn't able to come here himself, but he has delegated us to come here and speak with your wife."

Cora looked steadfastly at the floor.

"Sister, is it true that you used a cell phone in defiance of the *Ordnung*, and encouraged Mary Stoltzfus to do the same?"

"It *is*," said Cora, in a small, guilty voice.

Isaac broke in. "I found her cell phone, and destroyed it. I made Cora promise that she'd never use it again, and she has kept her word."

"That's good," Deacon King nodded. He turned to Cora.

"What do you say now, sister? The bishop asks if you repent of this disobedience, and if you are willing henceforth to obey the *Ordnung*?"

Cora lifted her eyes. "Oh, *yes*," she said quickly. "I *repent*!"

The deacon nodded. "That's good, very good."

"So we can return to the bishop with the news that you intend to conform to the *Ordnung*, and live quietly?"

"Yes, yes, *I promise!*" Cora breathed earnestly.

They looked at one another. "That puts our minds at rest," said Deacon King. "The bishop will be happy to hear that this matter is resolved. As long as there is no further incide—"

The sound of frantic pounding on the door cut him off. Isaac lifted startled eyes, and Cora bowed her head and hurried to answer it.

Fannie and Amos Stoltzfus stood panting on the landing.

"Cora Muller, if I find out that you had *anything* to do with this —" Fannie burst out, but her husband put a hand to her shoulder.

"May we come in?" he asked grimly.

Cora looked a query over her shoulder, and Isaac stood up. "Yes, please come in," he said, and motioned to the chair he had been using.

Cora hurried to bring more chairs, and Fannie Stoltzfus collapsed into the seat and put a handkerchief to her eyes.

The two ministers exchanged a startled glance.

Cora brought two folding chairs, and Amos Stoltzfus and Isaac sank gingerly into them.

"Sister Stoltzfus, we trust —" Minister Fisher began, but her wails drowned him out.

"Mary's gone!" she cried, sobbing. "She's run away. She's gone to the *English*!"

Everyone in the room absorbed this news in shocked silence. Cora rolled her eyes to Isaac's, and answered the urgent question on his face by shaking her head earnestly.

"She wasn't in her room this morning," Amos added. "She left us this note."

He handed the note to the deacon, who read it gravely.

"She says that *Seth Troyer* has gone with her," Deacon King muttered.

Cora closed her eyes, frowned, and mouthed silent words.

"Cora Muller, Elie Meissen told me this morning that she saw you eating lunch with Mary on the day she disappeared," Fannie gasped. "If you have any care for a mother's feelings, you'll tell me *where she went*!"

Cora gaped at her. "B-but I don't *know*!" she stammered. "*Really*! I met her in town, and she invited me to lunch, and we talked, but she never said a *word* about running away!"

"Did she give you any hint of where she might have *gone*?" Amos Stoltzfus urged.

"*No*! She never breathed a word! All she told me was that

she was going out with Seth. She didn't give me the *faintest* hint that she was even thinking about such a thing!"

"This is *your* fault, Cora!" Fannie sobbed. "If you hadn't encouraged her to talk to Seth Troyer on that cell phone, she wouldn't have fallen into his *clutches*, and she'd still be home today! Clearly, he was a little *wolf*, who amused himself by preying on innocent girls!"

"Fannie," Amos admonished her, *"remember where you are."*

"I can't help it," Fannie sobbed. "We've lost her, we've lost our daughter!"

Isaac tried to gain control of the situation. "Brothers, we'll do what we can to help," he said, casting an awed glance at Fannie's flushed face, "but maybe it would be better to ask Seth's parents where they might have gone. They might have a better idea."

"Yes, that sounds like a good idea," Deacon King added. "And I wouldn't despair, Sister Stoltzfus. Children often come back, when they find that the English world isn't all they had thought."

"I pray you're right," Fannie sniffed, and wiped her eyes. "But we've been going out of our minds with worry!"

"Let's bow our heads, and pray," Minister Fisher suggested. "For wisdom, and for safety for Mary and Seth."

Fannie and Amos nodded, and everyone bowed their heads. But Cora looked up at Isaac's face across the Stoltzfus' bowed heads. His eyes were wide and baffled and exasperated.

She shook her head, and shrugged, and lifted her hands.

After a few moments of silence, the deacons rose. Deacon King put his hand on Amos Stoltzfus' arm. "Is there anything we can do to help you find Mary?" he asked.

Amos shook his head and pulled his hand across his eyes. "Just *pray*."

He turned and led a sobbing Fannie out the door and down the stairs. The deacons turned in the doorway and shook hands with Isaac.

"We'll take Cora's answer to the bishop," Deacon King told him. "But you must understand, this matter is only closed if there is *no further trouble*."

Minister Fisher added: "The bishop instructed us to tell you that if we have to come back again, Cora Muller, you may expect stricter consequences."

"We understand," Isaac answered quickly. "There will be no more trouble."

"We're glad to hear it," Deacon King answered. "Good day, Isaac Muller. Cora."

They walked slowly down the wooden steps.

When the last echo of their footsteps had faded into silence, Isaac turned to Cora with his hands on his hips.

CHAPTER SEVENTEEN

"Isaac, I promise you, I didn't know a thing about it!" Cora said earnestly. She shook his arm. "Isaac, you have to believe me!"

He shook his head and sank down into a chair. He put his hands over his face.

"I believe you," Isaac said wearily. "It isn't your fault." He rolled his eyes to Cora's. "But you heard what they said, Cora. *One more mistake*, and –"

"Oh, Isaac, I know!" she said earnestly, "believe me, I'll never *look* at a cell phone again!"

"I don't want you to try to get in touch with Mary Stoltzfus, either," Isaac said softly. "I know she's a friend of yours, Cora, and I'm sorry. But we're on thin ice with the bishop. *No more trouble!*"

"Oh, I *promise*, Isaac," Cora replied quickly. "No more

trouble! But now I understand why Mary asked me to lunch," she added sadly. "She was saying *goodbye*, Isaac."

Isaac looked at her sympathetically, and put his arm around her shoulders. "I'm sorry, Cora. But it's plain that your friend was unhappy here. If she wants to live with the English, no one can stop her."

"I suppose not," Cora murmured. "I'm glad that at least she has Seth with her. They can keep each other company."

"That was *your* doing, was it?" Isaac asked, and his voice was faintly teasing.

Cora dimpled. "Mary didn't *like* Seth at first, but I did a few little things to build him up. And they must have worked. She ran away with him!"

Isaac's smile faded. "Yes, she did. Let's just hope the bishop is more understanding about that, than Fannie Stoltzfus."

"I feel so *sorry* for Fannie, Isaac," Cora said sadly.

He raised his eyebrows, and Cora added earnestly: "I know she sounded mean and harsh, but they were both *very* upset. I'm sure that Fannie will settle down in a little while, and we'll be friends again."

Isaac looked at her affectionately. "I'm sure she will."

"And now that we've gotten our official visit, Isaac, that means things are all right again – doesn't it?"

A faint frown clouded his face. "Only if there's *no more trouble*, Cora."

"Oh, there won't be, Isaac," Cora replied quickly. "No more trouble – I *promise!*"

***

Cora worked hard to be as good as her word: over the next few weeks, she walked softly, and made no waves. She and Isaac were too busy in any case: they had to clean the lower floor of their house, and it was an exhausting job.

Joseph brought Hezekiah and Jeremy over one afternoon, and they helped Isaac clear out the old furniture and lumber. They used Joseph's wagon to carry the huge load back to Gideon Miller's farm.

When they returned, Cora had a barbecue waiting for them in the back yard. Isaac made a picnic table out of some lumber and a pair of sawhorses, and they had carried folding chairs down from the living room. Cora loaded the table with barbecue pork ribs slathered in sauce, burgers, homemade potato salad and cole slaw, and corn on the cob, and biscuits, and green beans topped with bacon, followed by chocolate cake and custard.

Joe's boys had grown just since Cora had seen them last. Hezekiah's voice sounded an octave lower, and he looked at least five inches taller than she remembered. *He* was too dignified to play, but Jeremy still cracked jokes and jostled his brother and poked at Isaac, who swatted him playfully with one hand.

It was a happy day, and the boys kept her busy with their insatiable eating, but Cora noticed that after the meal, Joseph and Isaac drifted off to the corner of the yard and talked quietly. They stood there with their arms crossed, and she couldn't hear what they were saying. Joseph didn't give any hint of what they were discussing, but Isaac occasionally turned his head and looked at her.

Cora set the lemonade down on the table with a thump.

It was irritating to have a brother and a husband who apparently thought that they had to *manage* her. She was a grown, married woman, and she didn't need to be *discussed,* as though she was a child.

But Cora squelched that brief spark of irritation almost as soon as she felt it. She reminded herself that she was on probation, still very much under a warning from the bishop, and that she needed to curb her temper.

That visit from the bishop's representatives had been like a splash of cold water, and had been more real to her than all of Joseph's, or Mary's, or even *Isaac's* warnings.

Even the fury she'd felt against Leah Hauser had damped down under its chilling influence.

Cora bit her lip. Those two ministers had made her *feel* her danger: she was walking a fine line, and she needed to play it cool.

Luckily, Isaac's preparations for the opening of their shop kept her busy, and she was glad for the distraction.

Once the junk had been removed from the first floor of the house, they began working in earnest. Cora mopped the floors clean and washed the windows, and Isaac varnished the floors and painted the walls and the doors. After about three weeks of work, they had a clean, bright, bare showroom from which to sell furniture.

Then they moved on to *filling* all that empty space.

Three nights a week, Isaac rented out Gideon Miller's shop machines to cut and work pieces that he would assemble at home: beautiful heart pine bedroom suites, rockers, dining tables and chairs, desks, and bookcases.

Isaac made a little wooden desk and chair for her to use, and moved it into one of the little side rooms, and designated it their office.

On the nights when he wasn't in the shop, Isaac showed her how to work a little register that he had found at a garage sale. He studied about bookkeeping, and small business practices.

Most nights he collapsed in bed as soon as he came home from the shop, or fell asleep with a book on his chest.

And Cora would remove the book gently, and kiss him,

and turn down the lamp.

***

As the weeks passed, their showroom began to fill up with finished pieces. Isaac was a craftsman, and his work showed it: the furniture was smooth as silk to the touch, beautiful to look at, and as blonde and sturdy as he was himself.

"We need to start getting the word out," he told her one night.

The glow of a single lantern filled their bedroom with soft light. They were lying in bed, and as usual, Isaac had a book on his chest.

"Everyone in town already knows that we're opening a shop," Cora shrugged. "What else can we do?"

"We need to make sure that visitors know it, as well," Isaac mused. "And we need to be online. This house is wired for electricity," he mused. "Maybe I can talk to the bishop. Gideon Miller got permission for a phone line, and a computer, and a website for *his* business."

"But I don't know anything about the *internet*, Isaac," Cora objected.

Isaac looked at her ruefully. "Neither do I," he admitted. "For right now, I guess we'll have to start where we are. Cora, I want you to take those flyers we had printed up, and go to the businesses in town and ask to post them there. And we can ask at some of the places further out where the English tourists go."

"I will," Cora told him, taking the book from his chest. "But tonight, Isaac Muller, no more talk about *work*. I want you to go to sleep."

She put the book firmly on the nightstand, leaned over and kissed him, and turned out the light.

Isaac was out moments later but Cora stayed awake for a while, watching him regretfully.

Isaac *had* to do all of this, of course, to provide for them. And she knew that hard work was necessary, and right, and godly.

But she couldn't help feeling a little bit upset, because Isaac was too tired to do more than kiss her at night. They weren't on their *honeymoon* anymore.

Cora looked down and picked at the coverlet.

But she was also haunted by the fear that there was more to it than that. Because ever since Isaac had come back from the *Hauser's*, their love life just hadn't been the same.

She looked at him again, turned her mouth down, and rolled over.

CHAPTER EIGHTEEN

The next morning was bright and sunny, a good day for hard work. Isaac buried himself in the empty showroom, assembling furniture, and Cora's job for the day was to go from store to store in town, passing out flyers to whoever would agree to display them.

At midmorning, Cora had won agreement from most of the town shop owners that they would display the advertisements. But she hesitated outside Elie Meissen's store, because she was still mad at Elie for blabbing everything she knew and getting her in trouble with Fannie Stoltzfus.

Still, it was hard to be angry with Elie for long. She had no malice, and was absolutely fair: she blabbed *all the time*, and about *everybody*.

Cora entered the shop with a prayer on her lips.

Elie looked up as she entered.

"Hello, Cora Muller!" she beamed. "You look bright and shiny this morning! What brings you in?"

"I came to get some things," Cora told her, "but I also wanted to ask you if we could leave some flyers here about our new furniture shop. We're going to be opening it soon, and we wanted to get the word out."

"Yes, of course, Cora! Give them to me," Elie told her, and took a handful. "I'll put them here in the display rack, on the top row, where everyone can see them."

"Thank you, Elie," Cora told her gratefully. "We really appreciate it."

"Isaac does such beautiful work, I may buy something myself. Or tease Micah to buy it for me," Elie giggled.

"How is your husband, Elie?"

"Oh, he went to Marietta to visit his brother for a few days. I couldn't go, somebody has to mind the store, but in a way, it's kind of nice. Don't you dare tell him I said so, but Micah *snores* like a train whistle."

Cora looked down and put a hand over her mouth.

"Oh, Cora, and wasn't it a shame about Mary Stoltzfus!" Elie nattered on. "Her mother told me that she *disappeared* after she came to town that day. I thought she looked unhappy, poor thing. I wonder where she went."

Cora looked away uncomfortably. "I wish I knew, Elie,"

she murmured, and meant it.

"Her parents are beside themselves, of course. But I always had a feeling that Mary might surprise us all one day. It's the quiet ones, you know, that you have to watch! I just hope that she and Seth are all right."

"Yes, so do I," Cora answered. She didn't like the direction the conversation was going. It reminded her that she missed Mary, and that she was worried about her.

It also reminded her that she'd promised Isaac that she wasn't going to try to reach Mary.

That made her uncomfortable, too.

"I see that you have some fresh tomatoes in this morning, Elie," she replied, to change the subject. "I think I'll get some for Isaac, he loves them."

"Yes, feel free to browse, dear," Elie told her sunnily. "I'm here if you need me."

Cora smiled and drifted away from the counter, leaving Elie to greet another woman who had just walked in. She picked up a basket and browsed the aisles. Elie got the pick of the local produce, and her vegetables were always straight from the field. Her shelves were lined with sweet, robust jams and jellies made by local women, with fresh-baked bread, chow chow, pickles, apple butter, and homemade candy. The store always smelled of cinnamon tea and freshly ground coffee. It was a pleasant place to linger that morning.

Until something struck Cora from behind and almost knocked her down.

Cora threw her hands out to keep from smashing into a table full of tomatoes. When she had pulled herself upright again, she turned around.

To her amazement, Leah Hauser was standing there, with a wry smirk on her face.

"Oh, I'm so *sorry*, Cora," she trilled, laughing. "I wasn't paying attention. It's so easy to be distracted when there are so many nice things around," she added, looking over at Elie.

Elie beamed at her.

"I'm sorry that Isaac had to leave us so soon," she added, turning to Cora. "He's always *such* a help. Daed says to tell him that we'd be happy to have him back *anytime*."

"Isaac and Cora are opening a new store, Leah, did you hear?" Elie added helpfully. She waved a brochure. "They're going to be selling Isaac's furniture. He always makes such beautiful things."

"Oh, let me see that," Leah replied, and took one of the brochures from Elie's hand. "Well, well! That's good news! I'll be over when the store opens, Cora," Leah promised. "I need a new bed. Make Isaac can make one for me."

Cora turned her face to the wall and squeezed her eyes shut. She reminded herself fiercely that *Elie Meissen was standing there, the biggest gossip in the county,* and that she would repeat *everything she saw.*

"I just got finished telling Cora that I might make my husband buy one of his pieces for me," Elie nattered artlessly. "Isaac's furniture is so well made, it lasts forever."

Cora opened her eyes and turned to face Leah and Elie. She snatched the brochure out of Leah's hands and forced her lips into a smile.

"Yes, *everything* that Isaac makes *lasts forever,*" she assured them. "No one knows that better than *I* do."

She turned her smile in Elie's general direction. "Thanks for your help, Elie," she said evenly. "I have to get these out this morning – lots of other places to go."

"Good luck, dear," Elie smiled. "Not that I think you'll need it."

"Yes, Cora – *good luck,*" Leah echoed, and laughed. "Tell Isaac I said *hello.*"

Cora walked out quickly, and kept going. She walked down the street with her eyes on the ground, and her hands wrapped tight around the little basket.

She had to get home, and quickly, too. If she didn't, she was going to start screaming right in the middle of the street.

She closed her eyes and kept putting one foot in front of the other, not caring if she crashed right into a wall. She was so angry that the inside of her eyelids looked *red* instead of *black.*

The clatter of a buggy in front of her made her open her eyes again. She had almost walked out into the street.

She turned down the little side street that led back to their house and quickened her pace. A shriek was building inside of her, and she couldn't afford to let it go, not here, not where there were so many people to see and take word back to the bishop or the minister or whoever else was supposed to be *managing* her.

She dropped the little basket. Flyers went scattering through the air as she lifted her skirts and broke into a run. She dashed around a corner, down another block, and turned again into the little deserted street where they lived.

She dove into the tiny little side street beside their house, leapt onto the stairs, and ran up to the door without breaking her stride. She burst in, tore through the living room, threw open the bedroom door and flung open the window.

She stood there, panting, with her hands on the sill.

Then she squeezed her eyes together, balled her hands into fists, and screamed at the top of her lungs.

CHAPTER NINETEEN

The next Sunday was a worship Sunday. It dawned calm and bright, and by 7 o' clock, Cora and Isaac were almost ready to leave for church.

It had been several days since Leah Hauser had pushed Cora to the edge, and she had recovered her self-possession. She had said nothing to Isaac about the incident, and didn't *intend* to say anything.

It was *over*.

She made Isaac stand in the doorway until she had gotten his coat to hang just right.

"We're going to be late, Cora," he objected mildly, looking up at the ceiling.

"You're a businessman now, Isaac," she teased him. "You should look *neat*."

They walked down the steps, climbed into their buggy, and

clattered out into the street. As they slowly left the town behind, Cora's spirits rose. Worship was being held at Enoch Horst's farm. It wasn't all that far from town, but it was a nice drive on a fresh morning in early summer.

When they began rolling through the country lanes, Cora breathed in deep. It felt *good* to be out of town for a change.

"Do you miss it, Isaac?" she asked him wistfully.

He didn't have to ask what she meant. He looked at her and smiled. "Yes. I do. Maybe if the shop is a success, we can save some money and get a place of our own further out. We'd have more room there."

"Oh, I'd love that, Isaac," she agreed. Cora let her eyes wander out across the big fields. Faint green rows were visible as far as the eye could see, and the air smelled fresh and sweet.

It was good to be out of the house on a beautiful Sunday morning, and to be reminded of *God,* and of *calm, rational* things.

Cora stole a look at Isaac's profile as he drove the buggy. She hadn't told him about meeting Leah Hauser at Elie's store. She didn't want to see the worried look on his face again, or to give him the idea that she was going to make trouble.

She had needed to vent her feelings, after Leah had almost *knocked her down,* but even so, she had managed just fine without Isaac having to get involved.

After all, she told herself, Isaac didn't care about Leah Hauser, so it didn't *matter* what Leah said or did.

Mary had been right: she could afford to *play it cool*. And that was *exactly* what she was going to do.

***

When they arrived at the Horst farm, there was a fine turnout. The yard and the road outside were lined with black buggies. Cora scanned them, looking for Joseph and Katie's rig.

"Oh, Joes and Katie are already here," she noted, spotting it.

Isaac helped her down out of the buggy, and they walked hand in hand to Enoch Horst's barn, where worship was being held.

Benches were already set out in two neat sections: one side for the women and the other for the men. Cora squeezed Isaac's hand as they parted, and she went to find Katie.

Katie and Emma were sitting on the far right end of the last row, and Cora snuggled in beside Katie.

Katie welcomed her with a hug, and Emma leaned over to say hello. Dorathea was sleeping in Katie's lap like a little doll.

Cora and Isaac had arrived a little late, and worship was about to begin. The last stragglers were entering the barn and finding seats. Singing was about to start, and Cora reached for a hymnal.

The song leader announced the hymn number, and everyone turned to it. As Cora looked down, a late arrival sat down on the bench to her right and reached for one corner of her hymnal.

Cora looked up and stiffened.

It was Leah Hauser – *again.*

The song leader began singing the first line of the hymn, and the congregation followed. Cora stared at the hymnal without seeing it, trying not to let herself dwell on Leah's pious smirk.

She looked over at Katie, and her sister-in-law returned her glance with a smile. Cora bit her lip in frustration, thinking that Katie was as innocent as her sleeping baby. She knew nothing of what happened at the Hauser farm. *No one* knew -- except Leah and Isaac and – *herself.*

The hymn dragged on, five minutes, ten minutes. All of the songs from the ancient hymnal were extremely slow to sing. Cora stood up straight, and turned her head just enough to see that Isaac's startled eyes were on them, from where he stood on the other side of the aisle.

Cora twisted her lips down. She could only imagine what

he must be thinking. He was no doubt worrying that she was about to *explode*, about to make a *scene*, about to start pulling Leah's hair.

And he would be *right*.

She closed her eyes, praying. *Please God*, she prayed, *Help me to stay calm. Help me to remember what the bishop said. I can't afford to lose my temper, not here!*

She opened her eyes again, and Leah turned and smiled right into her face. Then she lifted her hand to the hymnal and began to trace an odd pattern across the page.

Cora frowned, wondering what the witch was trying to do. Was Leah going crazy, or was she merely trying to make her feel as if *she* was?

She followed Leah's finger as it circled back and forth across the page. At first it made no sense, but then the message became clear.

Cora flushed to the roots of her hair and suppressed a scream of rage by sheer force of will.

Because Leah's finger was circling between four words in the hymnal, over and over again.

Up to the top right of the page, to the word:

I.

Down to the middle of the page, to the word:

Know.

Over to the far left, to the word:

You.

Back to the middle again:

Know.

I know you know.

Cora ground her teeth and looked up at the ceiling. She tried to remember Mary's warning, those things she had said that had sounded so smart at the time, but the words scattered in the air and flew away like birds.

Cora could feel that Katie was looking at her, and her sister-in-law's eyes were concerned. Cora made an effort to control her expression. If *Katie* could see that she was upset, other people might notice, *too.*

Mercifully, the hymn finally ended.

Cora dropped her side of the hymnal and left Leah to grab for it as it fell from her hands.

CHAPTER TWENTY

Mary sat on a stool in Becky Thompson's big kitchen, peeling potatoes. Cooking was one of the few things she could think to do, that might help her earn her keep in the Thompson's bewildering house.

Strange lights flashed from every appliance in vivid shades of blue and green, and they beeped and squealed whenever she touched them, as though they were complaining. To add to her confusion, everything that Becky cooked seemed to come out of a box, in powdered form, or from a plastic jar.

Mary told herself that she'd never figure out how to cook in an English kitchen.

But at least she knew *potatoes.*

Becky walked in, saw her peeling the potatoes, and laughed.

"Mary, you don't have to do that," she chided. "You're a

guest here!" She opened the refrigerator and took out a jug of tea.

"I know," Mary shrugged. "But I feel lazy if I'm not doing something. And I want to help. I *owe* you."

"You don't *owe* us," Becky drawled, laughing. She looked at Mary's downturned face, and her laughter faded into a smile.

"I know what it's like," she added softly. "It's not easy to strike out on your own."

"How did you do it?" Mary asked, not looking up.

Becky sighed and poured out two glasses of tea. "I *didn't.* At least, not right away. The first time I left, I was about your age. Seventeen. I lived with an English friend for a few months, but I couldn't find work and came back home.

"I tried again when I was nineteen. That time, I stayed out for six months. I found a job working for an elderly lady, but then she fell ill, and I came back again.

"The last time, I was twenty-one. I had a job and a place to stay all lined up before I left. I had a friend come pick me up in her car, in the middle of the night.

"I never went back."

Mary stopped peeling.

"*Ever?*" she asked, in a small voice.

Becky put the glasses of tea down on the table. "I tried visiting my parents a couple of times," she said softly. "I could tell they were glad to see me, but it was awkward. Because by that time, I had married Ben, and they knew that I was never coming back for good.

"That was hard for them," she sighed, looking up at the ceiling. "*Very* hard."

"Do you still see them?" Mary asked.

"Not so much," Becky replied, with a pained smile.

"That's what I'm afraid of," Mary confessed quietly. "That my parents won't want to see me again."

"You can never tell," Becky told her. "They might. But you have to be prepared for the possibility that they might not."

"I know."

"But I still want to be *here*," Mary added suddenly, looking up. "I couldn't live there for the rest of my life. I just never fit in, you know? I like to read and to write and to travel and to meet new people.

"I *still* believe in God. But I know Mamm and Daed will be worried about that part. They have their own ideas."

"And you have yours," Becky agreed. "And that's *okay.*"

She handed Mary a glass of tea. "Now stop peeling

potatoes and come and help me. I need someone to hold my bag while I go shopping."

Mary looked up, and Becky laughed and took her arm.

***

They piled into Becky's little car, a red VW, and drove out to the local shopping mall.

"Now, before you can find a job, Mary," Becky was telling her, "we need to get you some work clothes. Something you can wear in a business environment. What kind of job are you going for?"

"I don't know," Mary replied. She suddenly felt *very* green. "I can cook, and clean, and write, a little. I used to teach school, and I speak French."

Becky cruised the lot, looking for a parking place. "We'll get you some nice comfortable work clothes. Some sneakers, and some khakis, and a polo shirt. And a pair of dress slacks, and a nice solid top, and some business flats."

She shot a glance at Mary's face. "And a few outfits for Friday night," she grinned. "I can see that there will be *boys*."

Mary flushed and looked down at her hands.

"Of course, Seth will probably object, but it won't do him any harm to know he's not the only game in town," Becky teased, and Mary couldn't keep from smiling -- just a little.

"Where *is* Seth?" Mary asked. "I haven't seen him since breakfast."

Becky pulled into a parking space. "Ben took him out to the boonies. He's going to try to teach him how to drive a car," she laughed. "It *will* take a while."

Mary imagined Seth driving a car. For some reason, she wanted to laugh.

"Of course, we'll teach you, too. You're going to need to learn how to do that. But we'll take things one step at a time."

***

Mary had never been to a shopping mall before. It was worlds away from the little shops at home that sold cloth rather than finished clothing, and also different from the small, quaint fashion boutiques that she had visited in Paris.

It was huge, and bright, and crowded, and incredibly *noisy*.

Mary looked at the mannequins in the store windows as they walked past. They were dressed in skin-tight, low-cut clothes, often in neon colors.

She stared at a mannequin that was draped in a see-though blouse. She wanted to dress English, but — she would never be able to wear *half* of what she was seeing.

The mall was like some high temple of *hochmut*, with every jangling necklace and low cut dress screaming "look at me!"

Becky glanced over and read the thought right off her face. She laughed.

"Yes, I know. But don't worry, Mary. We'll find you something you'll be comfortable wearing."

Mary shot her a grateful look, and then rolled her eyes, and her silent thanks, up to the high ceiling.

CHAPTER TWENTY-ONE

On Sunday morning Becky and her husband Ben prepared to go to their church. Mary watched them as they bustled around the kitchen. Ben was in a dark blue suit and tie, and Becky was wearing a pale green suitdress.

"You're both welcome to come with us," Becky said, for the millionth time.

Mary looked over at Seth.

"I don't think so, Becks. But thanks," Seth assured her, smiling.

"Well, there's all kinds of stuff in the fridge, if you get hungry. We've been invited to a church luncheon, so you guys will have the house to yourself until about one or two. You can watch television if you get bored. We did show you how to get the pay channels, right?"

"Yes. You did," Seth assured her.

"Well, then, we'll be back in a little while." Becky sighed and pecked Seth on the cheek, and waved to Mary.

Ben took her arm, and they walked out the door.

After the sound of their car engine had faded down the street, Seth turned to her.

"Come on," he said.

They walked out into the back yard. The Thompsons had a huge, manicured back yard, mostly shaded by gigantic oak trees. The mottled shade beneath them was a pleasant place to sit on a sunny summer morning.

Seth led Mary to a little swing under one of the oaks, and they sat down together. He reached for her hand, and they swung back and forth, gently, for a long while.

Finally Mary said: "It feels weird, you know?"

Seth nodded. "I know. It feels like we should be at worship now. Everybody *else* is."

Mary twisted her mouth. She could see them in her mind: her parents, and Seth's parents, and the bishop, and their neighbors. Her school children and their families. Even Cora, and her big, blonde husband. All of them were sitting in someone's barn, with their heads bowed, singing.

Right this minute.

"Becks is nice to ask, but I couldn't go with them," Seth

confessed. "I don't even know what a Lutheran *is*."

"It wouldn't feel right," Mary agreed. "It's too soon." She turned to him. "Are you still going to become a Mennonite?"

"I don't know. Maybe. But I don't know any Mennonites around here."

Mary looked down at her feet. "I'm scared, Seth," she whispered. "I don't *know* what I believe now."

He put his arm around her. "We're no different, Mary," he told her firmly. "We're still the same as we were a few weeks ago. We just live in a different place, that's all."

"Do you – do you think God is *mad* at us for leaving, Seth?"

Seth raised his brows. "No. I don't think God is like that. It's our parents who are upset, Mary."

Mary blinked back tears. "I miss them so bad, Seth. It's funny, when I was at home, they bored me to death and I thought they were so old-fashioned. But now I wish I could talk to them again. Even if they yell at me."

Seth was silent for a while. "My parents called me last night," he said at last.

Mary looked up at him quickly. "What did they say?"

Seth shrugged. His expression looked *controlled*.

"They said to come home."

"Did they ask where we are?"

Seth nodded. "I didn't tell them, though. Because my Daed would come here. And it would make no difference. And that would be a waste."

"Did they – did they tell you anything about my folks?" she asked quietly.

He nodded. "They said your parents are worried. I told them we're okay. That they don't need to be worried that we're in trouble, or starving, or something."

"Thank you," she replied, in a barely audible whisper.

"I told them that I was going to go to school, and be an engineer," Seth murmured. "And that I wasn't coming back."

Mary looked at Seth again. There wasn't a flicker of emotion in his eyes, but she knew what he was hiding.

She squeezed his hand.

"*I'm* not going back, either," she said.

The sea breeze ruffled the top of the oak tree, tossed the branches, and made the swing rise in the air slightly, and fall again. Seth turned and kissed her, and hugged her tight. They sat there, holding one another, for a long time.

"Just because we've moved, doesn't mean that we've *changed,* Mary," Seth repeated, and she nodded in agreement.

"I *haven't* stopped believing in God," he muttered.

He was silent again, and then began to sing, slowly and sonorously:

"O Gott Vater, wir loben Dich…"

Mary felt quick tears spring to her eyes, but quickly joined in:

"Und Deine Guete preisen,

Das Du Dich, o Herr, gnaediglich,

An uns neu hast beweisen,

Und hast uns, Herr, zusammen g'fuehrt,

Uns zu ermahnen durch Dein Wort,

Gieb uns Genad zu diesem."

Seth fell silent, and bowed his head. Mary joined him in prayer, and they prayed for a long while.

But when Mary finished, and looked up, she sensed motion out of the corner of her eye. She looked over to the right.

To her embarrassment, a frankly curious neighbor was standing on the other side of the fence, watching them. He had been watering his lawn, but he was just standing there, staring at them, as the flowing hose quickly created a pool around his feet.

CHAPTER TWENTY-TWO

"The first thing you do when you get into a car is to put your seat belt on."

Mary was sitting in Becky Thompson's car with her hands on the wheel. She looked a question, and Becky lifted up her own seat belt, and demonstrated.

"Now let me see you do it."

Mary suppressed a sigh and pulled the seat belt over her chest and clicked it into the slot.

"And how often do you do this?" Becky pressed.

"*Every time*," Mary repeated dutifully.

"That's right. Now put the key in the ignition and crank the car, like I showed you."

They were sitting in the middle of an abandoned parking lot outside of town. Grass and weeds were growing through cracks in the concrete, and the pavement wasn't perfectly level. The lot was part of an abandoned subdivision project that had been cleared, and leveled off, and then left to slowly deteriorate.

It was a strange place for a driving lesson, Mary thought, but it had one big plus. Whatever mistakes she made in this parking lot would be completely *private* ones.

"Now, you turn the car using the steering wheel. It's pretty simple. Turn it left, to go left, and turn right, to go right. Let me see you turn right."

Mary pulled the wheel to the right.

"Good. Now, you make the car *start and stop* by using the pedals. You stop the car by pressing the left pedal with your foot. And you start the car by pressing the right pedal. Let me see you start the car."

Mary pinched her lips together in determination. She jammed her foot down on the right pedal, and the engine roared. The tires squealed and the VW catapulted across the pavement, over the edge of the lot, down a slope, and deep into an overgrown meadow.

The car bumped to a stop. When Mary looked out the window, she couldn't see because the weeds were higher than the car. She turned to Becky with a pounding heart.

"I – I'm sorry, Becky," she stammered.

Becky looked over at her with wide eyes, and nodded. "Not so *hard* on the pedal the next time, Mary," she replied.

***

Becky cleared the desk in front of Mary and clicked a button. The little dead laptop jumped to life. The screen winked white, and then blue. Mary watched in amazement as Becky's flying fingers pulled up page after page of text.

"Now, the GED is going to be a challenge, Mary. There are lots of resources online that you can use to study for it. I'll pull them up and print them out for you.

"Since you like to write, and you speak three languages, the language arts and writing portions shouldn't be hard for you, but you're also going to be tested on social studies, math, and science. You'll need to study hard for those. I'll help you, if there are parts you don't understand, and you and Seth can help each other. He's going to be taking it with you."

Mary nodded.

"A GED will make it much easier to get a job, and to get into college. Do you plan to go on to college, Mary?"

Mary looked up at her, and went red.

"I want to be a writer," she said simply.

"Then you'll need to go on to school," Becky nodded.

"Maybe you and Seth can go to the same place."

Mary looked down at her hands. She'd been so focused emotionally on *leaving home*, that she hadn't bothered to game out any of these important issues. Now she felt like a fool for overlooking them, and wondered if Becky thought so, too.

She must look like a complete *greenhorn*.

But to her relief, Becky didn't seem like the sort of person to make her feel her ignorance. She was a kind, giving, generous person, and Mary was heartily glad that she had agreed to come with Seth.

She couldn't imagine what she would have done, if she'd left *alone*.

***

"Now, the secret to makeup is to enhance your looks without making yourself look overdone. Like this."

Mary was sitting in front of the big mirror in Becky's bathroom. Becky leaned over and penciled a faint, fine outline over one of her eyebrows.

"Take a look." She handed Mary a hand mirror.

"See what it does? It makes your brows look defined, but it's not obvious."

Mary turned her head and nodded approvingly. To her

amazement, she liked it even better than the dramatic makeover she had been given in Paris. It was just as attractive… but more like *her.*

"You're a lucky girl," Becky observed, tilting her head. "Your complexion is nearly flawless. You don't need foundation. Just a little touch up here and there with concealer, and not much of that." She dabbed at Mary's face with a little brush.

"I'll give you just a touch of color with the blush brush. You have a nice dusky coloring, so I'll go with something like a deep peach."

She took a little brush, dipped it in a little jar of powder, and whisked it over Mary's cheekbones. Mary closed her eyes and giggled like Cora Muller, because it *tickled.*

Becky stepped back and assessed her handiwork. "Yes, I *like* that. Now, all you need is a little sheer lip color. If you were going out for dinner or something, I'd do lipliner too, but for daytime just a swipe of something sheer should be enough." She uncapped a little tube of shiny lipstick and painted it carefully over Mary's lips.

Then she stepped back again. "Oh, *Mary.* Take a look at yourself."

Mary raised her eyes. A stylish young *English* woman was looking back at her.

"You're beautiful," Becky smiled.

Mary looked at herself in amazement. For the first time in her life, she *felt* beautiful.

The young woman looking back at her wasn't Mary Stoltzfus, the Amish bookworm, or Mary Stoltzfus, the rebel who returned from Paris with black hair.

The woman in the mirror was the Mary Stoltzfus she had always wanted to be – stylish, beautiful, and ready to join the world.

She looked up at Becky, and smiled, and put a hand over her mouth. Tears filled her eyes.

Becky looked down at her sympathetically. "Yes, I know," she said softly, and hugged her.

CHAPTER TWENTY-THREE

The next weekend Becky announced that she and her husband were going to the beach.

"And *you're* coming with us," she told Mary and Seth, as they sat in the kitchen for breakfast.

Mary looked over at Seth with a faint smile. She knew Becky and Ben well enough by now to know that whatever they had planned would be something *good*.

"We've all been working way too hard for the last few weeks. It's time for a day off," Becky added.

Mary and Seth exchanged another wordless look. Seth lifted his shoulders ever so slightly. Mary didn't know what Becky was talking about, and to judge from his expression, neither did Seth.

Since they'd come to the Thompson's, their workload seemed trifling, almost *decadent,* compared to their former

RUTH PRICE

chores.

But Seth smiled, and said they were looking forward to it.

They all piled into the sedan. To Mary's surprise, Becky opened the door and allowed the golden retriever to climb in. She rolled the window down and he climbed up at once to stick his head out of it as they rolled out of the driveway.

"We're going to have a lobster boil," Ben announced, as they drove. "Have you kids ever had lobster?"

Seth shook his head, but Mary replied: "I did once, when I was in Paris. It was delicious."

Seth leaned over and whispered in her ear: "What is it?"

Mary drew a blank. She shrugged. "I can't explain it," she replied softly. "You'll just have to see it for yourself."

***

They drove down to the ocean. As Seth had once told her, it was very close. The sun was out, and the light sparkling off the sea made Mary's eyes hurt until Becky passed back a couple of pairs of sunglasses for them to wear. "Be sure to put on sunblock," Becky added, tossing a tube into the back seat. "Put a layer on every inch of skin that isn't covered up, if you don't want to end up as red as a pair of lobsters yourselves!"

They drove down to a bluff overlooking the ocean. Ben parked the car, and unpacked the trunk. Together they carried

148

two big umbrellas, folding chairs, a huge pot, and a cooler down to a nice secluded spot on the white sand.

Mary shaded her eyes. The water was blue and sparkling and smelled of salt and fresh air. The gulls wheeled overhead and cried stridently.

Ben showed Seth how to set the umbrella, and helped him open it. It unfurled to a huge round canopy, providing ample shade for two chairs and a table.

Soon they were reclining in the shade with their feet propped up. Mary watched in delight as little sailboats plowed through the blue water, and gulls danced on the wind, and very faint and far off, the huge gray freighters crawled across the horizon.

She had never seen anything like it in her life.

She looked over at Seth. He was wearing a pair of faded blue jeans and a green tee shirt and a baseball cap that he'd turned backward.

That, and the sunglasses, made him look almost like a stranger.

Mary looked at him and wondered why it had taken her so long to see that Cora had been right: Seth really *was* a handsome guy.

He wasn't big and tall and muscular, like Cora's husband, but he was on the high side of average, and had nice broad shoulders and a lean physique. He had decent biceps, even if they weren't huge, and nice brown hands with long, sensitive fingers.

He had a square jaw, and a beautiful white smile.

He was even getting to be a better kisser. Though, to be honest, the bar was set pretty low in that area. For the *both* of them.

He looked over at her and smiled.

"What?"

She hesitated, and then decided to go for it.

"Oh, I was just thinking that you're a pretty hot little chili pepper," she said blandly. "And I was wondering if you'd like to go for a walk."

Seth sat bolt upright in his chair and laughed. "*What?*"

"You heard me."

Seth grinned in delight, and spread his hands out in appeal to his cousin. "How can I turn down an invitation like *that?*" he asked.

Becky and her husband were looking at him, and were hiding their hands behind their mouths.

"Oh, you two have fun," Becky replied faintly. "Just remember where we are."

Mary picked up a baseball cap of her own, tucked her hair underneath it, and stood up. Seth kicked out of his shoes, and she kicked out of hers, and they walked barefoot to the waterline, and away from their friends.

"I was wondering when you were finally going to wake up to my manly qualities," Seth told her, looking out over the ocean. "Was it my bulging muscles" – he flexed his arm for her – "or my winning smile?"

"Oh, it was lots of things," Mary replied, smiling. "You *sneak up* on a girl."

The tide came in suddenly and slapped spray over them. Mary squealed and laughed as the brine splashed up on her face. She licked the salty taste off her lips.

A million tiny crabs disappeared into the sand as they approached. A larger and bolder one raised its claws menacingly as Seth's bare toes passed by.

"So, if I'm such a chili pepper, why are my hot little lips not getting a kiss?" Seth asked, and looked over at her.

Mary laughed, and leaned over, and kissed him as thoroughly as she knew how. It felt right, somehow, with the breeze ruffling his hair and the sun on his shoulders and the cool waves lapping their feet.

Seth put his arms around her and pulled her to his chest. He lifted her cap off her head and let his hands wander in her hair.

And the thought occurred to Mary that she might feel more for Seth Troyer than just admiration, and lazy attraction.

Maybe it was because she *had* no one else. Or maybe it was because he was always surprising her with his courage. Or maybe it was just because he had long lashes and *really* nice eyes.

But the kiss she gave Seth Troyer, while the gulls screamed all around them, was a kind of question. She was testing her own feelings.

Because she was perfectly secure in the knowledge that she never had to test *his*.

CHAPTER TWENTY-FOUR

Seth released her, and they joined hands again, and they walked down the beach all the way to the lighthouse, a good mile and a half from where they'd started. They walked in silence, until Mary eventually said:

"I'm *so* glad I came with you, Seth. I don't know what I would've done if I'd run away alone."

He squeezed her hand, and said nothing.

"And your cousin and her husband have been amazing to me. *Really* amazing."

"Ben and Becks have saved our lives, that's all," Seth said quietly.

"I've kind of wondered -- *why* are they so good to me, Seth?"

He looked over at her. "What do you mean?"

"I mean, why are she and her husband going to all this trouble? They've done way more for me than I ever expected. To tell you the truth, I feel kind of *guilty*," she confessed, kicking at a mound of sea foam. "They're *your* relatives. I don't have any connection to them at all. I feel kind of like a nuisance."

Seth stopped and took her by the shoulders. "You're not a nuisance, Mary," he said earnestly. "And you *do* have a connection to Becky. I'm her cousin, and you're – you're my *girlfriend*."

Seth tilted his head slightly. As if he was watching to see if she'd accept this new title.

Mary opened her mouth, and thought better of opening it. She suppressed a smile.

"Your girlfriend, huh?"

"That's right."

She couldn't suppress the smile any more. She looked out over the ocean again, grinning.

"I see."

"But Becky would be just as nice to you if you *weren't*," he told her. "She and Ben are just really good people. Plus, they never had children, so it might be that they're – kind of getting all that stuff *out*, when they help us.

"Don't let her know I said anything -- but Becky got real

sick when she was young. Her parents took her to an English doctor, and he cured her, but he said that she'd never be able to have any children."

"*Oh.*"

Mary fell into an awed silence. Big families were very important to Amish couples. Few things were sadder than an Amish man or woman who couldn't have children.

And Mary felt that she suddenly understood why Becky had left. The life she would've lived -- as a childless Amish woman – was kind of like the one she *herself* had been facing.

"It was an open secret in the family," Seth went on. "We didn't tell anybody else, of course, but I remember my parents talking about it."

Mary digested his words thoughtfully. "I won't repeat it to anyone, Seth," she replied. "But I can't go on living with your relatives *forever*," she added. "We've been here for weeks. They're probably *praying* we'll leave!"

Seth shook his head. "If that's what you think, you don't know them," he sighed. "Becks and Ben just *like* people. They entertain all the time. Having people in their house is *normal* for them. But I *totally* agree with what you're saying," Seth added quickly. "We definitely need our own place. We need to get jobs, and start making money."

Mary looked up at him. "*We?*"

He looked away from her, and went red. "You know what I mean."

"No... I *don't*."

He sighed. "I don't know where I'm going to be living, but wherever it is, it's going to be close to where *you* live," he explained patiently.

"Oh." She swung his hand in hers, and smiled. "I thought you were asking me to live with you, or something."

Seth went red again. "No, not that."

Mary smiled and let it go. But it was plain to her that Seth *was* thinking in terms of them living together, once they got jobs. And she knew he was telling the truth when he said he wasn't just going to ask her to *move in*.

Mary bit her lip. There was only one remaining explanation.

Seth was, apparently, already thinking about *marriage*.

She looked at him out of the corner of her eye, and the thought suddenly came to her that maybe -- just maybe – *that* explained why Becky and her husband had opened their arms so wide to her, had trained her to drive and to dress and to do so many other things that no one else would normally have done.

She wondered if Seth had described her to them as his *future wife*.

The thought filled her with something almost like panic. What if he suddenly asked her to *marry* him?

And what if she wasn't *ready* to marry Seth? What if she decided that she didn't want to marry Seth *at all*?

If the Thompsons were expecting her to say *yes*, and she *didn't*, they'd naturally feel that she'd hurt Seth, and they might push her away.

If that happened, it could mean that she'd be on her own again. And then, she really would be adrift.

She'd have *nobody*.

Mary stared at the ground, and watched as the waves slapped back and forth.

She knew that Seth was an honest guy. He wouldn't deliberately lie to her, or scam her. And it was most likely that the explanation he'd given her was the right one: Becky and Ben were an open-hearted couple who liked people, and who didn't have children of their own.

They would naturally open their home to Seth, and to her, since they were doing exactly what Becky had done herself, years ago. They might even feel a few parental emotions towards them – who knew.

But if Seth had told them that she was his future *wife*, it would explain a lot of things that didn't make much sense otherwise.

Mary didn't want to believe it, but the suspicion settled down in her mind and refused to be stirred.

"I think it's time to turn back now," Seth smiled, pointing to the lighthouse.

She gave him a long, searching look, but the sunglasses kept her from reading his eyes.

"Yeah – I think we've gone too far," she agreed, and didn't look at him again.

CHAPTER TWENTY-FIVE

Joseph Lapp took off his hat and stepped into the parlor of the Hottstetler farmhouse. The 100-year-old building was the home of Bishop Hottstetler, the highest-ranking church leader in their district. His venerable home had been the scene of many historical events in the life of their church, and had an almost iconic reputation in the district.

The big, two-story house was very plain, and made of white clapboard. The ancient floorboards creaked underfoot as Joseph crossed the room. The light streaming in through the windows looked slightly distorted, because the glass was hand blown, and dated from before the Civil War.

Bishop Hottstetler was sitting at a small table with papers scattered across its surface. The table, and the chair he was sitting in, were practically the only furnishings in the room.

He adjusted his glasses and looked up.

"Come in, Joseph Lapp," he said softly.

Joseph entered the room gingerly. He knew that he had to watch his step in more ways than one.

"Please – sit down."

Joseph slowly lowered himself onto a small leather couch facing the older man. He sat ramrod straight.

"I hear that you want to talk to me. What can I help you with this afternoon, brother?"

Joseph's bright blue eyes found the bishop's. "I want to make a confession," he said.

The bishop took off his glasses and cleaned them with one cuff. "I see. Does it have anything to do with your sister, Cora, and her trouble?"

"Yes, it does."

The bishop looked at him mildly. "Your sister has already made her confession. She says that she repents of using the cell phone, and that she will not use it again. I consider the matter closed. Do you have something else to add?"

"I do."

"Tell me, then."

Joseph kept his eyes on the bishop's. *"I gave Cora the phone."*

The bishop's bushy gray brows rose. *"You?"*

Joseph nodded. "I gave it to her before she was married. As a way to reach out for help, if she needed it."

"So, am I to understand that you own one, too, Joseph?"

Joseph nodded stiffly. "For the same reason."

The bishop sighed and put his glasses on the table. "You understand why cell phones are against the *Ordnung*, Joseph. They are a link to things in the outside world that corrupt and ensnare."

Joseph nodded. "Yes. But they are also a link to things we may *need*." He leaned forward slightly. "If Cora had been able to use a cell phone when she was with that man who abused her, then she could have called us, and we could have come to *get* her. She would have been spared injury and pain.

"When my wife had her trouble, when she was suffering in her mind because of her grief, and we were worried about the baby, I came to understand that we needed a way to *reach help quickly.*"

The bishop gave him a direct look from his bland green eyes. "Brother, we must trust that the *Lord* will help us, when we need help. The Lord does not need a cell phone to deliver us from trouble."

Joseph nodded. "That is true, bishop. But cell phones are only good or bad, depending on how they are *used*," he replied earnestly.

"There are ways to restrict what is seen on a cell phone. They can be powered by solar chargers, so that electricity would not be necessary. We might approve only the kinds of phones without cameras, or internet connections. They can be adapted to be *useful* -- not harmful."

The bishop was silent.

"My brother-in-law, Isaac Muller, has just opened a furniture shop in town. He will soon be coming to you to ask permission for electricity, and a phone line, and an internet connection for his business, like many other businesses in our district. The church has come to understand that these things are necessary to make a living. Perhaps the church might consider that a cell phone can be useful for every day, as well.

"I have come to confess my own part in this thing, bishop. And I will submit to the ruling of the church. But I also request that the church revisit this issue. I respectfully request that the church *reconsider* the limited use of cell phones."

The bishop was silent for several minutes. The sound of a bee butting the window pane outside sounded loud in the stillness.

Finally he replied: "I know that some of our youth on *rumspringa* are using cell phones. I know that many of our adult members are likely doing so in secret, as well." He looked up at Joseph. "Though you are the first to *admit* it."

He strummed his fingers on the table. "Do you repent of

this disobedience to the *Ordnung*, Joseph Lapp?" he asked.

Joseph bowed his head, and nodded.

"Good. Then I will bring the issue up again at the next council meeting. We will discuss it again, and see what the people say. Until then, I will keep your cell phone."

Joseph took off his hat, reached into it, and handed the bishop the phone. The bishop turned it over in his hands, studying it, and set it down on the table.

He looked up at Joseph, and a faint smile dawned across his face.

"And you can tell your young brother-in-law that he can use the electricity and other things. *Only* for the business, mind. It must not be used in the portion of the house that is his *home*."

"Thank you, Bishop," Joseph replied gratefully. "He will be very thankful."

"I've watched that boy," the bishop commented, "and he works very hard. He should do well. But he also needs all the help that he can get."

Joseph looked at the older man, nodded in rueful agreement, and rose to take his leave.

CHAPTER TWENTY-SIX

Joseph went directly from the bishop's farm to the newly-minted Muller Furniture Shop in town. Thanks to a month of backbreaking work, the crisp white building was as bright and shiny as a new penny and open for business. The windows shone, the house was freshly painted, and even the sidewalk outside the house was spotless.

A little bell tinkled as Joseph opened the front door.

Isaac looked up from the gleaming pine counter that they had installed. Behind him, a brightly lit showroom was filled with sturdy, well-made furniture: bookcases, desks, bedroom suites, dining tables and chairs, and rockers.

"Hello, Joseph." Isaac cracked a white grin and gestured to the space around him. "What do you think?"

"It looks good," Joseph nodded. "*Very* good."

"We've had some browsers already," Isaac told him in

quiet satisfaction, "and two buyers. A desk and a rocking chair."

"I'm proud of you and Cora. You're off to a flying start," Joseph told him approvingly.

"We'll start repaying your loan at the end of this month," Isaac promised.

Joseph waved him away. 'There's no rush, Isaac. I'm satisfied. It looks like you're going to do well. The bishop thinks so, too."

"The bishop?" The smile faded from Isaac's face. "Did he *call* you?"

Joseph shook his head. "No, I went to see *him*. It was a private matter. But while I was there I told him that you'd be asking for permission to use electricity and a landline and an internet connection for your business. He gave his approval. He said you were a hard worker, and that he looked for you to do well."

Isaac's bright eyes shone. He looked down, trying to hide a smile.

"Where's Cora?" Joseph asked. "I was hoping to see her, while I was here."

Isaac nodded toward the ceiling. "She took a break from the counter, so I'm covering for her. She's upstairs, making lunch."

"I think I'll go up to see her."

"She'll be glad to see you. It's through that door and up the stairs."

"I remember."

Joseph nodded, and disappeared through the door to the little side room. The sound of his feet were clearly audible through the wall, as he climbed the steps, emerged in the little hall at the top of the stairs, and walked into the living room.

The sudden sound of Cora's delighted squeals, and her excited voice, wafted down faintly from upstairs. Joseph's deep, indulgent laughter followed.

Isaac smiled and shook his head. Cora adored her big brother, and the practical result for *him* was that he could probably forget about getting his lunch for at least thirty minutes, and very likely more.

His thoughts returned to Joseph's news. The bishop's blessing on electricity and internet use was going to be big for them. Now they could build a website, advertise online, build a catalog. Ordering materials and parts would be easier and...

The tinkling of the little bell interrupted his excited thoughts. Isaac lifted his eyes.

But his hopeful expression quickly darkened at the sight of the new arrival. It was Leah Hauser. He set his mouth into a tight line.

"What are you doing here, Leah?" he asked quietly.

She walked up to the counter and leaned over it. "I came to see *you*, of course," she answered, smiling. "Have you thought about what I said?"

"You need to leave, Leah. I have nothing to say to you."

"Nothing, Isaac? Are you *sure*?"

"I'm sure. Go away and leave us alone."

"Where's Cora?" Leah asked, looking around. "I had hoped to see her, too."

Isaac met her eyes grimly. "Leah, I saw what you did at worship that Sunday, and I'm not going to stand for it. *Stay away from Cora.*"

Leah shrugged and pouted. "Don't be unfair, Isaac. It was the only seat left. Believe me, I didn't want to sit next to your wife, any more than *you* wanted it."

The sound of Cora's laughter wafted down faintly from above stairs. Leah lifted her head.

"Oh, is Cora home?" she asked lightly.

Isaac looked at her grimly. "Leah, if you try to make trouble, I'll go to the bishop and tell him everything that happened. I don't *want* to do it. But I *will*, if you don't go away."

"*Everything*, Isaac?" she asked, with an innocent

expression.

Isaac's face flushed a deep, dull red. But he met her eyes.

"It won't be pleasant," he replied evenly. "But if you don't go away and *leave us alone*, you're going to find yourself at his house."

"Don't be mean to me, Isaac," she replied, in a lower voice. "Is it a crime to love you? I can't help it, you know," she whispered. "I haven't stopped thinking about you ever since –"

"Leah –"

"I just want you to know that I still feel the same. I will always love you, Isaac, no matter *how* cruel you are to *me*."

Isaac sighed and looked away.

"I cried all night," she said softly. "You can't understand what that's like, Isaac, to *love* someone, and to have no *hope*."

She leaned close. "But I can live even without hope, Isaac," she breathed. "I can live on *anything* you're willing to give me. Come to me, Isaac, even once. I can live on it for the rest of my life!"

Her dark eyes were wide and beautiful and pleading, and her pink lips were pulled into a rosebud pout.

Isaac looked at her, and thought that she was beautiful.

But the sight of her stirred nothing in him now but anger, and a lingering pity.

"Go home, Leah," he said quietly. "The answer is *no*."

She pulled back from the counter and frowned. Then her eyes returned to his in a final appeal.

"Please don't hate me, Isaac," she whispered. "Because I'd do anything, risk anything, for *you!*"

Cora's laughter floated down from above. Leah's expression twisted.

She turned and fled, leaving Isaac to close his eyes and exhale a long, deep breath.

But his eyes still followed her, as she hurried down the street and disappeared around the corner.

***

It was only minutes later that Joseph and Cora came down the stairs, arm in arm.

"Are you sure you won't stay to lunch?" Cora asked her brother.

Joseph shook his head. "I have to get back. My work is piled up as it is." He turned to Isaac and slapped him on the back. "Congratulations to the two of you. This is a fine shop. I'll bring Katie back with me the next time we're in town. *And* the wagon, because I'm sure she'll see something here that will make me *need* it."

"I'm going to tell her you said so," Cora teased. "Tell her hello for us, and the children. Kiss Dorathea for me!"

Joseph put up a hand in parting, and walked out.

Cora watched him affectionately as he left. "Joes is *so* sweet," she sighed.

Isaac raised his eyebrows. "I'm here, *too*," he reminded her.

Cora laughed and turned to him. "Yes, you *are*," she agreed, and leaned across the counter to kiss him on his brow, and his cheeks, and his nose.

She stepped back and took his big jaw in her hand. "Are you hungry?"

"*Starving.*"

"There's a roast beef sandwich and some soup, and chips and pickles, and some potato salad, set out on the table."

His face fell. "Is that all?"

"And some macaroni and cheese, and some pie," she replied absently, and bent down to pick something up off the floor.

"Why, who left *this* here?" she laughed. She twirled a little piece of paper between her fingers. "It looks like a phone number," she murmured. "Did we get an English customer?"

The blood drained from Isaac's face. "We had a customer while you were gone," he replied evenly. "It must have fallen out of their pocket. Here, give it to me, I'll throw it away."

"Oh, I'll keep it," Cora shrugged. "It could be important. They might come back for it."

"There's probably no need."

"Oh, run on, Isaac," Cora laughed, and slapped at his hand. "I know you're hungry. Stop thinking about business. *Go eat your lunch.*" She tucked the little slip of paper in her apron.

Isaac's hand fell to his side. He looked back at Cora over his shoulder, as if he wanted to say something, before he turned and walked up the stairs to their apartment.

CHAPTER TWENTY-SEVEN

Cora sat down on a little stool and settled in behind the counter. It had been an uneventful day except for Joe's visit. She had spent most of it sitting behind their counter, watching people pass by.

Their street was off the beaten track, but occasionally people did cut through on their way to somewhere else. Mostly locals, because they were the only ones who knew the short cut.

Cora propped her chin on her hands.

The other side of the street was occupied by an old brick building. It had been a drug store in the 20's, and had been run by an English businessman. A faded cola advertisement was still barely legible on the side of the building.

Now it was empty. There were four little windows in the wall, all dark.

The sidewalk in front of the building was also old. Little plants were sprouting up through the cracks in the cement.

There was a tall elm sapling in the little strip of grass between the sidewalk and the street. A little robin had built a nest in the topmost branches, and it hopped back and forth on the grass, catching ants.

For a long time, that was all the excitement that Cora could see outside.

Occasionally a buggy rumbled down the street. Cora waved to Obadiah Glick as he drove past, and he threw up a hand in greeting. The Glicks were distant relatives of the Mullers, though Cora had forgotten just how Obadiah was connected to Isaac's family.

The afternoon wore on. An English couple wandered in and asked about a desk and a chair for their den. She showed them several of Isaac's desks, but they left without making any commitment.

After lunch, Isaac retreated to the little shop area in the back yard. He had made himself a work area, with a bench and a cabinet for his tools. She could hear him back there, banging away at something with a mallet.

Cora returned to watching the street.

Another buggy suddenly came rolling past. It was moving slowly, and the woman sitting in it turned her face toward the front of the shop. Cora sat up suddenly. It was Fannie and

Amos Stoltzfus.

Cora had only gotten a fleeting glimpse of Fannie's face, but her expression was one of patent misery. Her sad, swollen eyes went through Cora's heart like an arrow, and she wondered fretfully if Mary's parents had gotten bad news about her.

Cora's mouth drooped. Poor Fannie!

She couldn't blame Mary for leaving, though. She had been ready to do that *herself*, once. If she hadn't fallen in love with Isaac, she might very well have run away, too.

But she still missed her friend. She had been able to tell Mary things that she couldn't tell anyone else. Things that even *Isaac* might not have understood.

She wondered if Mary was in trouble. Of course, Seth was with her, and that helped a little, she supposed. But if she was really honest, she'd have to admit that Seth was just as likely to *need* help, as to *give* it.

She twisted uncomfortably in her chair, and the little scrap of paper fell out of her apron. She placed it on the counter absently.

Then her mouth fell open. Her eyes returned to it.

The scrap of paper reminded her that *she still had Seth Troyer's cell phone number*. It was still upstairs where she had hidden it, in a little canister of baking soda.

Cora bit her lip. It was true, she *had* promised Isaac that she wouldn't call Mary.

But she had never promised not to call *Seth*.

She turned and looked back over her shoulder. Isaac would probably be unhappy with her, if he found out, but she really *did* want to know what had happened, and maybe she could reach Seth and find out.

She thought about Fannie's miserable face, and pulled her lips down.

"Isaac, can you take over for a few minutes?" she called suddenly.

The hammering stopped. There was a small pause. Then Isaac's voice responded from far in the back.

"Yes."

"I won't be gone too long," Cora promised. *"But I need to run an errand."*

Isaac appeared at the back door. He looked intently at her face.

"I promise, just a *few* minutes," she smiled.

He nodded, and put the mallet down.

Cora turned, ran up the stairs to their apartment and dodged into the kitchen. She opened the little canister of baking soda and shook the powder off of the little paper.

Then she pinned it to the inside of her apron, and skipped down the back steps and into the street.

The town library had a little room with a private telephone. If she was lucky, she could get it without having to wait for anyone else.

CHAPTER TWENTY-EIGHT

Cora closed the door to the little room behind her and sat down in the library cubicle. She lifted the receiver off the hook and dialed Seth's number.

Her heart beat faster as the phone rang.

"Hello?"

"*Seth!*" Cora cried. "It's Cora Muller!"

"Oh, *hi,* Cora," Seth's voice answered.

He *sounded* happy, and that was a hopeful sign, anyway.

"I just remembered that I still have your number, and I – I just wanted to check and make sure that you and Mary are okay."

"Oh, we're fine," Seth assured her. "We're staying with friends, and they're spoiling us beyond belief. We're studying for our GEDs, and Mary and I just got our driver's licenses this week."

"Oh, Seth, how *exciting*," Cora answered, momentarily distracted by this news.

"We went to the beach the other day and had a picnic, and we've even got some job leads. Mary is going to be tutoring a neighbor kid in French, and Monday will be my first day working as a lawn mower. Only until we can pass our GEDs, and apply for college, of course."

Cora dimpled in delight. "I'm so *glad*, Seth," she told him fervently. "I just wish I could talk to the two of you more often. I really miss you."

"We miss you, too, Cora," Seth replied ruefully.

"Everybody was very... *surprised*," Cora said carefully.

"It was what we both wanted. It's going to work out, don't worry."

"I know it's for the best, but – I wish I could talk to you guys."

"How are you talking to me now?" Seth laughed. "I thought you were busted!"

"I *am*," Cora made a face, "I'm calling you from the library." She brightened. "But if it's okay with you, Seth, I'd like to call back sometime, because Isaac and I are opening a furniture store and we're allowed to have a phone for the business. I might sneak and call you sometime."

"*Do*," Seth replied quickly. "It's *so good* to hear from someone at home!"

There was suddenly a rustling noise. Cora was delighted to hear Mary's voice in the background.

"*Is that Cora?*" she was asking.

There was a jostling sound, and the sound of Seth laughing.

"Bye, Cora," he said quickly, "she's taking the phone away from me!"

Mary's voice replaced his in the receiver.

"Cora?"

"Oh, Mary, I'm so glad to get ahold of you!" Cora cried. "*Why* didn't you tell me that you were leaving? I was shocked out of my mind! *And* worried," she added. "Seth says that you guys are okay?"

"We're great," Mary replied. "It's good to hear your voice."

"Everybody in town was knocked right off their pins when you left," Cora told her. "Me, too! You sure kept your own counsel, Mary Stoltzfus!" she laughed.

"Yeah, I guess I did. I just didn't want anybody to get in trouble," Mary confessed. "How – how are my folks?"

Cora sobered instantly. "I saw them today, Mary," she

replied softly. "They were driving down our street. Your mamm looked very sad."

There was no sound on the other end.

"Mary?"

"I'm still here. Tell me – tell me what happened with you and Leah Hauser. I hope you took my advice?"

Cora snorted. "You were *right,* Mary. She *is* trying to yank my chain. But I think I'm okay now, because the ministers came by our house, and asked me if I repented, and I said *yes,* and they said *good.* As long as I, you know – reform."

"What did Leah do to you?" Mary asked.

"You won't believe it. She sneaked up behind me in Elie Meissen's and shoved me so hard that I almost *fell down.* She tried to play it off by saying it was an accident, but I knew she meant it. It was all I could do not to clock her, right there in front of Elie!"

"It's a good thing you didn't, though," Mary said thoughtfully. "You *didn't* – did you, Cora?"

"No, I didn't, you would have been proud of me. But I had to run all the way home and scream for a while," Cora confessed.

"*Mm.*"

"Oh, and then she sat down right next to me at worship –

can you imagine the nerve? – and she kept pointing to words in the hymnal. Guess what they spelled out?"

"I can imagine."

"*I know you know,*" Cora replied indignantly. "Sometimes I wonder if I'm going to make it!"

"*And that's the point, Cora,*" Mary said quickly.

"What do you mean?"

"Don't you see what she's doing, Cora? She's *daring* you. She *wants* you to fight her, like you did in the barn that time.

"Because you're *already* standing on the edge of a cliff. Leah knows that if she can get you in big trouble *again*, you're going over the edge. You'll be shunned for sure. Your husband won't be able to even speak to you, much less –"

Her voice trailed off.

"And if she can get you and Isaac *separated*, then she'll hit him again. When you're not around -- when he's lonely and upset."

Cora's mouth fell open.

"You have to think of something to get rid of her, Cora. Sooner or later she'll do something so bad that you'll lose it. And then she wins."

"I think she knows that Isaac doesn't love her," Cora murmured glumly. "But that doesn't seem to even *matter* to her."

"Well, one thing's for sure," Mary replied. "If you want to live there in peace, *with your husband*, you're going to have to *get rid of her* somehow."

"I don't even know where to *buy* a gun," Cora grumbled.

"I'm serious. You have to *think* of something. Because everybody has a breaking point. All Leah Hauser has to do is find *yours* -- and it's game over."

"Oh, I don't know how to get rid of her," Cora complained, "Though heaven knows, I wish I could! I wish *Leah* was the one who ran away, not you and Seth!"

"What did you say?" Mary asked.

"I said I wish *Leah Hauser* was the one who ran away!" Cora replied.

"Cora, that's a *great* idea," Mary said, with surprising earnestness. "Maybe you can make that happen."

"How?"

"I think I know. But you have to do *exactly* as I say."

CHAPTER TWENTY-NINE

"You need what?"

Cora stared at Elie Meissen's round face and patiently repeated: "I need some yarn. Isaac is going to my brother's on Friday to help him build a shed, and I wanted to send the yarn to my sister in law. She's the one who just had the baby, you know." She sighed. "Isaac will be gone *all day Friday*. I'll have to manage the store without him!"

"I'm sure you'll do fine," Elie assured her, and scratched her head. "But I don't know if we have yarn in stock right now," she explained. "Let me look!"

She bustled to the shelves, rummaging through the closest things she could find, but came up empty.

"I don't think we have it, sweetheart," she admitted ruefully. "I'm sorry."

"Oh, dear," Cora murmured, looking down at her feet.

"Well, thank you for looking, anyway, Elie. I always like to visit your store first!"

Elie beamed at her, and she waved, and walked out of the store. But when she got well away, Cora smiled to herself.

Now the *entire county* would know that Isaac was going to be gone, all day long, on Friday.

Including Leah Hauser.

On Friday morning Cora saw Isaac off. He stood in the doorway of their apartment, holding the mighty lunch box that she had packed full of sandwiches. Of course Katie would feed him, but Isaac *always* needed something for the road.

She stood on tiptoe, kissed him, and watched him leave.

Then she cleaned up the breakfast dishes, made herself tidy, and walked downstairs to open the shop.

It was a bright, cloudless summer morning, and Cora unlocked the shop doors, opened the register, and seated herself behind the counter.

Business was somewhat more brisk than it had been during the week: she sold a pair of side tables to an English couple, a small desk to Eli King, who needed it for his wife's notions shop, and one of Isaac's beautiful hall trees to a young woman who said she was doing research for a book.

When lunchtime came, Cora pulled her own little lunchbox out from underneath the counter, and ate a small meal.

She hadn't seen any sign of Leah Hauser all morning, but Cora was confident that she wouldn't pass up the opportunity to pick a fight – especially when Isaac wasn't there to prevent it.

Lunchtime passed, and a few more browsers came in. One of them bought a small clock, and another a desktop bookcase.

Traffic fell off in the afternoon, and Cora had to fight the impulse to nod off. The afternoon sunlight streaming in through the windows made her feel warm and drowsy.

But still there was no sign of Leah.

By four o'clock Cora began to be worried. She was counting on Leah's predatory instincts, but if she didn't show up soon, Isaac would come back home, and all her plans would be ruined.

The hands on the clock crawled toward five. Cora was beginning to think that she had misjudged her adversary, when the little bell tinkled -- and Leah walked in.

Cora assumed a placid expression. She was determined not to let Leah provoke her.

"What brings you here, Leah?" she asked, in her best helpful tone.

"Oh, I just thought I'd come in and browse," Leah said, breezing past Cora. "So, this is where Isaac works."

"It's where *we* work, yes."

"I see I'm the only customer," Leah noted, running her finger along a bookcase. "I hope you haven't been too lonely."

"Oh, I'm *never* lonely, Leah," Cora told her blandly. "Isaac is always so sweet."

Leah smiled sourly. "I'm curious. How do you live with him, knowing what you know?"

Cora bit her lip and looked down. "I don't know what you mean, Leah."

Leah shot a glance at the door. There was no sign of anyone on the street.

"I mean, did Isaac tell you what happened when he came out to our farm?"

Cora raised her eyes. "Yes, he did, Leah," she replied coolly. "I know all about it. He said that you tried to seduce him, and I believe it. He also told me that it didn't work, and I believe *that*, too."

"I see. I guess it wouldn't have been quite as tidy to tell you that we had a *lot* of fun together that night."

Cora met her eyes grimly, and then looked down again.

"It's a sin to try to seduce a married man, Leah," she said quietly. "I'm *disappointed* in you. But Isaac has *never* lied to me, and I know *he* was telling me the truth."

Leah laughed. "What do you *expect* him to tell you?" she asked scornfully. "Isaac is a nice guy, and all of that, but no man is *that* pure."

"I trust my husband," Cora replied, in a cracking voice.

"He told me that he was *exhausted,* because he was *always* having to get you out of trouble," Leah drawled.

In spite of Cora's best efforts, that shot went home. Her face drained of color. She closed her eyes, and took a deep breath, and gathered her strength.

"That's a spiteful thing to say, Leah Hauser. And it isn't true."

Leah tilted her head, assessing the look on Cora's face. She frowned.

"He said that you're a *drag* on him," she continued, "and that he feels *guilty* about it, but that – he really wishes now, that he hadn't *married* you."

"That's not true," Cora said, in a small voice.

Leah pressed in. "*Isaac told me that he loves me.*"

Cora squeezed her eyes shut, and went red, but countered evenly: "No, Leah. Isaac walked ten miles in the middle of the night to get *away* from you."

Leah's arm shot out and she slapped Cora full across the jaw. The force of the blow knocked Cora's cap off her head and caused her hair to come spilling out across her shoulders.

Cora sat there, breathing heavily. Then she raised her head, pulled her hair back from her face, and met Leah's eyes.

"Violence is a sin, Leah," she replied calmly.

Leah's eyebrows rushed together. "What's going on?" she growled. "Why won't you *fight?*" A sudden premonition of disaster seemed to seize her, and she swept the showroom with her eyes.

A blinding flash dazzled her.

"Smile big, Leah," Mary Stoltzfus drawled, and stepped out from behind a bookcase, holding her cell phone aloft. "Because you're a star. I just uploaded the whole movie to the Internet. Who says that technology can't be useful."

Leah rounded on Cora. "You wouldn't *dare*," she growled. "You're one scandal away from *excommunication!*"

Cora smiled grimly.

"It's not *my* cell phone, Leah. And it's not *my* scandal."

"You know, if I were you, Leah," Mary mused, "I'd consider going to the English. They don't care *quite* as much if you chase married men, while the bishop – well, he takes a different view."

Leah went white to the lips. "You're bluffing!" she spat.

Mary shook her head.

"If you're still here tomorrow morning, Leah," she said softly, "you're a stupid girl."

Leah backed toward the door. Her hand found a little clock on top of a table, and she hurled it at Mary's head as hard as she could. The clock smashed off a bookcase an inch from Mary's head, and Leah fled out the door and disappeared.

Mary picked up the clock and put it back on the table. But Cora raised her eyebrows and whistled soundlessly.

"Remind me never to make you *mad*, Mary," she murmured, with an awed look.

Mary gave her an amused glance. "Well, Cora -- *now* we're even," she said.

CHAPTER THIRTY

"I brought this hoping that it would come in handy," Mary said, pulling a bottle of champagne out of her backpack. "It's the same kind of wine I had in France. You've *got* to try it."

The shop below was closed for the day, and they were sitting in the kitchen. Cora set out a pair of glasses.

Mary filled them, and then lifted her own. "To Leah Hauser," she said solemnly. "May she find love at last."

"*Far away from here,*" Cora agreed, and they clinked glasses.

She took a sip, and wrinkled her nose. "It's *good*, Mary! But the bubbles *tickle*," she laughed.

"I love this stuff," Mary admitted. "That's probably one of the reasons I'm with Seth right now. He took me out on a picnic and got me *beschickert* on champagne."

Cora put a hand to her mouth and giggled.

"I think Leah is finally out of your hair, Cora," Mary added. "Did you see the look on her face? I'll be surprised if she still lives here tomorrow."

"Did you really do what you said?" Cora asked curiously. "Upland a movie?"

"*Upload*," Mary corrected. "And no, I just saved it. I doubt I'll even need to use it. But if she makes trouble, just call me."

"Oh, Mary, I can't thank you enough," Cora replied, and squeezed her hand. "I don't know what I would have *done*, if things had gone on the way they were!"

"Enjoy your blonde farm boy," Mary told her fondly. "Tell him hello for me."

She drained her glass, and reached out to hug Cora.

"Oh, Mary, you're not going already?" Cora wailed. "I wanted you to have dinner with us!"

"I've got to go," Mary replied softly. "I have one other place to be before nightfall."

Cora hugged her, and rested her head forlornly on Mary's shoulder. "Do come back and see us, Mary," she begged. "And call. I miss you when you don't."

"I will," Mary promised.

"And be kind to Seth," Cora added softly. "He lo-- he *likes* you so much."

Mary smiled, and kissed her cheek, and shouldered the backpack. "I have to get that car off the street outside," she sighed. "I don't think it's supposed to be there."

She handed Cora a slip of paper. "Here's my number. Call me anytime."

"*Good luck, Mary.*"

Mary smiled crookedly, hoisted the backpack, and walked down the back stairs. Cora went to the door, waved, and watched as Mary climbed into a little red VW, cranked the motor, and drove down the street.

Cora sighed, and shook her head. And then she dimpled and looked up at the ceiling.

"I know I probably should apologize, Lord," she confessed, "but I'm not good at *letting it be*. Maybe You were the One who *let it be*, this time. *Thank you.*"

While she was standing there, she caught sight of a familiar figure on the street outside. It was Isaac, walking home.

She waited for him at the top of the landing. "Are you tired?" she asked sympathetically.

"Bushed," he nodded, giving her the empty lunchbox.

She put an arm around his waist and walked him back in.

He took a look at the kitchen table and raised his brows.

"Are we celebrating?" he asked, lifting the half-empty bottle of champagne.

Cora smiled. "Mary Stoltzfus was here today," she told him. "She gave us a *gift*."

***

The next morning, when Isaac opened the shop, the local customers were abuzz with gossip.

"It's like an epidemic," Josiah Ebert said solemnly. "First Seth Troyer, and then Mary Stoltzfus, and now Leah Hauser! All of them, running away like horses out of an open gate! We're glad to have *responsible* young people like you and Cora in town, Isaac!"

"What do you mean?" Isaac frowned.

"Why, haven't you heard? Leah Hauser just up and *bolted* last night! She left her folks a note that said she was going to stay with their people in Ohio. I'll wager it was the first that any of them had heard of it!"

Isaac raised his brows. "First I've heard of it, *too*."

He turned his head and looked at Cora with a suspicious glint in his eye. She returned his glance with an expression of wide-eyed innocence.

"No one had any idea," Josiah muttered, shaking his head.

"You just never know what people are *up to* these days."

Isaac was still looking at Cora. "No, you *don't*," he agreed.

After Josiah had finished his business, and gone his way, Isaac turned to his wife.

"What happened while I was gone yesterday, Cora?" he asked, arms crossed.

"We had a *good* day," she assured him. "We sold a hall tree, and a clock, and lots of other furniture."

"I see. Lots of customers visiting the shop?"

"*Mmm.*"

"Leah Hauser wouldn't have been one of them, by any chance?"

Cora raised her eyebrows, and shrugged, and sputtered. "I – I suppose she *might* have dropped by. There were *lots* of people here yesterday, Isaac, you can hardly expect me to remember *every* one."

"And Mary Stoltzfus was here *too*."

"Yes," Cora admitted.

"And she brought us *champagne*."

"*Mmm.*"

Isaac shook his head and looked down at the floor, and then up at Cora's face.

"I don't know what the two of you got up to, Cora," he sighed. "And I'm not going to ask any questions. I'm just grateful to God that it *worked*."

CHAPTER THIRTY-ONE

It was dusk when the red VW pulled up to the Stoltzfus farm. The house had already taken on the faint bluish tint of twilight, and the windows glowed gold.

Mary closed her eyes and rested her head against the wheel of the car.

Seth had offered to come with her, had been worried. His expressive eyes had been dark, full of concern.

He had been afraid she might not come back.

And as she looked up at her parent's porch, she had to admit that Seth had been right to be worried. In spite of everything she wanted, and everything she knew, the longing to run up the steps and fling herself into her parents' arms swept over her with such ferocity that she doubled over with it.

But she fought it down, because she wasn't going back.

Anything that gave her parents that impression would be cruel.

She gathered her strength, and opened the door of the car. She knew they had seen her, were probably watching her now. Cars were a rarity on the back roads.

She walked slowly up the steps, and paused in front of the door.

But before she could knock, the door burst open. Both her parents were standing there.

They stared at one another for an instant, and then Fannie burst out, "Oh, baby!" and pulled her into her arms.

Mary stood quietly as her mother cried over her, and her father patted her back.

"Thank God you're all right, Mary!" Fannie sobbed. "We've been going out of our minds!"

Mary looked down at her feet. "Can I come in?" she asked quietly.

Fannie burst into laughter. "Oh, of course you can!" she cried, and pulled Mary inside.

Both of them followed her as she sat down in a chair. They sat beside her, one on each side.

"We're so relieved, Mary," her father said. "We worried something might have happened to you."

"I'm sorry," Mary said, in a small voice. "I didn't want you to worry. I'm fine. Seth and I have been staying with some friends of his, and they've been wonderful. We have everything we need."

Fannie shook her head in confusion. "Everything you *need*? But – but you're coming back *home*, aren't you, Mary?"

Mary looked down. "No, Mamm. I'm not."

Fannie blinked at her, uncomprehending, and turned to her husband, as if for an explanation.

"I came here because I knew you'd be worried. I wanted you to know that *everything is okay*. I have a place to stay, and plenty to eat, and I'll be starting work soon."

Her father leaned forward, his eyes on her face.

"Then you're not going to join the *church*, Mary?"

She shook her head.

"Oh, Mary," Fannie cried, and put a hand to her mouth. "How can you turn your back on God, and on your family -- and your *home*?"

"I'm not turning my back on any of those," Mary replied, and looked up at her mother. "I still love God, and this place, and – and both of *you*. But I can't live here, Mamm. *I can't.* I don't fit in here, and we all know it.

"I want to go to school. I want to be a writer, and I need to go to college, to learn how."

Fannie's eyes brimmed over. "Oh, Amos, this is my fault," she cried. "I would *never* have let her help me at the school, if I'd known how it would affect her!"

"You don't have to go to college to be successful *here*," her father said brokenly. "It's a submissive heart that the Lord loves."

"I know," Mary replied. "And I will still go to church, and still follow God." She took his hand. "I will always love you, and Mamm. And I will always come back, as long as you'll let me."

She looked down again. "I hope you'll let me."

Amos Stoltzfus' eyes hardened. "It was that boy who did this to you, isn't it, Mary?" he asked indignantly. "That *Seth Troyer*, with his buggy rides and his picnics? He was the one who filled your head full of this nonsense."

"No, Daed." Mary shook her head. "Seth is like me, and we think the same way, but he had nothing to do with this. It was my decision. I would have done it without him."

"And to think I encouraged you!" Fannie cried, and pulled out a handkerchief. "I thought he was a fine, upstanding young man. And all the time he was plotting to lure you away from us, and from the church!"

"Seth *is* a – a fine, upstanding young man," Mary stammered. "He's just not an *Amish* man." She lifted a hand and brushed a tear off her mother's cheek.

"Any more than *I* am an Amish woman."

"I don't believe it, Mary," her mother protested. "This isn't like you. You're not yourself. You're under the spell of that *wretched* boy, God help you, and that's why you're talking nonsense!"

She lifted brimming eyes to Mary's face.

"Come home, darling. We'll never speak of it again, we'll forget it ever happened. If you want to teach, why, why, I'll go to the school board. I'll use my influence, and you can come back. Things will be the way they *always* were."

"Oh, Mamm," Mary said sadly, *"I'm so sorry."*

Fannie looked at her husband, and his arms reached for her. She buried her face in his chest and poured out her grief.

Amos held her, and looked at the floor, and nodded. "If this is how you feel, Mary, then you know what that means. You have turned your back on your faith, and your home, and everything you were taught."

"Daed –"

His voice cracked. "I will not have you coming here, upsetting your mother, and breaking her heart with your rebellion."

"I never joined the church, Daed," Mary replied desperately. "I never broke *any* vow. It's not the same!"

"If you can come back with a repentant heart, and a willingness to follow God, you know that we will welcome you with open arms. But as long as you persist in this rebellion, it, it –" he coughed, and wiped his eyes, "it would be better, if you stayed away."

Mary looked down, and nodded. She rose.

"I know you still love me," she said. "I still love you. I hope that someday you'll understand. I just wanted to let you know that I'm okay. I'll write. I'll –"

She broke off. She had reached the limits of her voice.

Fannie's muffled sobs were the last sound she heard, as she closed the door behind her and walked out to the car.

Mary cranked the car and turned on the lights and pulled the VW out onto the road. She wondered briefly what Becky would have thought, if she could have seen her.

Somehow, she was keeping the car in the road, at night, *and* while she was crying.

CHAPTER THIRTY-TWO

It was one o' clock in the morning when Mary finally pulled the car back into the Thompson's driveway. The front of the house was dark. Only one lonely light was burning in the foyer.

Mary pulled herself wearily out of the car. She stuck the keys into her pocket, and wiped her nose, and looked up at the sky. It was pitch dark, moonless.

She stumbled to the door and put her hand on the knob, but the door opened without her.

Seth was standing there, his sad eyes on her face. He opened his arms, and she went into them.

"I know," he soothed, stroking her hair. "Bad, huh?"

"Oh, Seth, it was awful," she sobbed. "I *broke their hearts*. I *hate* myself!"

"It's not your fault," he whispered, kissing her ear. "And

it's not theirs. You just believe differently, that's all."

"They blame *you*, Seth," she told him. "If you can *believe* that."

Seth turned his face down to catch her eye. "So, I have *influence*. I can live with that," he teased, and Mary sputtered out a laugh in spite of herself.

"That's what I like to see," he smiled, putting a finger on her lips. "Come on into the kitchen, I saved you a plate. It's lasagna night."

Mary looked up at him gratefully, and thought to herself that it was a lucky thing for her that Seth Troyer was *shy*.

Because if he had asked her to marry him, at that moment, she would have run away with him all over again.

End of Book 5.

Thank you for Reading!

I hope you enjoyed reading this as much as I loved writing it! If so, look for the next book in the series in eBook and Paperback format.

And if you are interested, there is a sample of the next book in the next chapter.

All the best,

Ruth

LANCASTER COUNTY SECOND CHANCES 6

CHAPTER ONE

"Oh, there it is! But why is their business hidden away on this dowdy little back street?"

The young couple, a pair of twenty-something tourists, paused on the sidewalk outside the Muller Furniture Shop. It was a two-story clapboard building, sparkling white with a neat black door and trim. The windows gleamed, the brass street number and door knocker shone, and the small patch of lawn between the shop door and the street was bright with red roses.

"It looks like something from 200 years ago, Paul," the woman breathed. "Just like on their web page. The Amish are so--*historic*."

She took his hand and they strolled across the street to the door. As they opened it a little bell tinkled overhead and the fragrance of freshly worked pine wood greeted them.

A beautiful blonde woman in Amish dress was standing behind a massive counter. A few wispy tendrils of shining blonde hair escaped from underneath her white cap. Her face was void of makeup, but her complexion was fresh and flawless, in spite of it. She lifted her big blue eyes to them and smiled tentatively.

"Welcome to our shop," she said softly.

The young man smiled, taking in her appearance. *"Hi."*

His female companion stepped forward and slid a hand across his shoulder. "We saw your website and thought we'd drop in while we were in town," she said briskly. "We are interested in the unfinished pine library desk."

The young Amish woman dimpled winsomely, and the young man smiled back.

"Yes, that's one of our most popular pieces," she agreed. "My husband is here today, he can show it to you.

"Isaac?" she called, "we have customers."

There was a faint clattering sound from the back of the shop, and presently a young giant emerged from among the bookcases. He was over six feet tall, with white-blonde hair and clear sky-blue eyes. He was dressed in a simple white shirt with rolled up sleeves, suspenders, and plain black slacks – but the way he filled out those simple garments would have made them fashionable on any runway in the world.

The young woman's mouth fell slightly open, and as her hand slipped from her companion's shoulder she pulled her sunglasses down her nose.

The young Amish man gazed down at them. "I have three finished desks right now," he told them. "Come and see."

He turned, and the two customers exchanged a wordless look before they followed him to where three beautiful, handcrafted pine desks were on display. The woman ran a hand admiringly over the silken surface.

"My, you are talented," she drawled, "it's as smooth as a baby's bottom! And *sturdy*," she added, smiling up at him. "It looks like it weighs a ton!"

Isaac nodded. "I make them to last. Here we have the unfinished one, but I can add any finish you want." He motioned to a small booklet of available finishes, and the man picked it up and flipped through the swatches.

"I think it's perfect the way it is. What do you think, Paul?" the woman asked, her eyes still on Isaac.

Her companion put the booklet down. "It looks good," he agreed. "Do you deliver?"

"Yes. For a little extra locally and more if it's out of state."

The man turned to the woman. "What do you think?"

"I love it," she replied, pulling out a drawer. "It's not like anything I've seen at the big-box showrooms."

The man turned to Isaac. "We'll take it."

"Good," Isaac nodded. "If you have a truck, I can help you load it. If not, we'll deliver."

The man looked at him as if he'd lost his mind. "We'll have it *delivered*," he responded faintly.

"As you like."

Cora greeted them at the front desk. "Did you like the desk?" she asked politely.

"Yes, we're getting it." The man reached into his wallet and handed her a card. "You can have it delivered to this address."

"We'll have it to you within a week," Cora told him dutifully. "And thank you, we appreciate your business!"

The two customers looked at each other again, smiled and took the receipt she offered them before leaving.

When they had stepped out into the street again, and the door had closed behind them, the man exhaled soundlessly. "Man, did you get a load of Hercules?" he marveled. "Did I want to help him *load the desk*?" He gave an incredulous crack of laughter.

The woman twirled a tendril of her hair. "Yes, he was a healthy specimen, all right," she agreed. "I wonder what they feed 'em out here? I'll bet *that one* could have moved the desk all by himself."

"Hey!"

"I'm just saying," she shrugged.

"And his wife!" the man went on, "right out of central casting – the little Dutch doll!"

The woman shot him a sharp glance. "Yes, I saw you staring at the milkmaid," she agreed. "All she lacked was a pair of wooden shoes."

The man grinned at her. "Yeah, she sure had *everything* else," he teased.

"Oh, shut up, Paul."

"Jealous?"

"*Mmm* – no. Because if you tried to flirt with her, she'd most likely shoot you down. The Amish are very repressed sexually. They're *religious*, you know."

"Yeah. Kooks, like all of those Bible thumpers."

They paused on the sidewalk, looking out toward the main town square. Several buggies clattered down the street, and here and there, Amish townsfolk mingled with shopping tourists.

"It's like taking mushrooms, Paul," she marveled. "I keep thinking I'm seeing things, but it's real."

He yawned. "I'm getting hungry. Isn't it getting close to lunch? Let's find a café, or whatever they have here."

His companion smirked and eyed him. "Yeah -- maybe we can find out what to feed *you*, to make you grow big and strong like *that* guy."

She jerked a thumb back toward the shop, and the man pushed her a little as they walked – perhaps in jest, and perhaps not.

CHAPTER TWO

As soon as the door closed behind their English customers, Cora turned to Isaac, hands on hips.

He looked down at her in amusement. "What's *that* face for?" he asked mildly. "Didn't we just sell a desk?"

"The way that English woman was staring at you, reminded me of Leah Hauser!" Cora objected. "I like to be polite to *everyone*, but some things make my hands tingle!"

"I would hate to have to explain why my wife just slapped a customer," Isaac agreed, sliding his arms around her waist from behind. "It would be *hard*."

He leaned down and kissed her ear. "Maybe we should

close for lunch. It's been a busy morning, and we both need a rest."

Cora closed her eyes. "Oh, I'd *love* that, Isaac," she replied fervently. "Just to have some time to ourselves, for a change!"

But the tinkling of the little bell announced that they had new arrivals. Isaac straightened, and Cora stepped away from him. She put a hand to her cap.

"Welcome to our shop," she smiled. "How can we help you?"

Thank you for Reading!

I hope you enjoyed reading this as much as I loved writing it! If so, look for the next book in the series in eBook and Paperback format.

All the best,

Ruth

ABOUT THE AUTHOR

Ruth Price is a Pennsylvania native and devoted mother of four. After her youngest set off for college, she decided it was time to pursue her childhood dream to become a fiction writer. Drawing inspiration from her faith, her husband and love of her life Harold, and deep interest in Amish culture that stemmed from a childhood summer spent with her family on a Lancaster farm, Ruth began to pen the stories that had always jabbered away in her mind. Ruth believes that art at its best channels a higher good, and while she doesn't always reach that ideal, she hopes that her readers are entertained and inspired by her stories.

FIC   09/13/2016   3CLY002/74/
PRI

Price, Ruth
Second Chances # 5

FIC   09/13/2016   3CLY002/74/
PRI

Price, Ruth
Second Chances # 5

DATE	ISSUED TO

B.W. P.D.   D B

Clay County Public

Library

116 Guffey Street
Celina, TN 38551
(931) 243-3442

J G

CPSIA information can be obtained
at www.ICGtesting.com
Printed in the USA
LVOW04s0715110916
504099LV00011B/103/P

9 781515 376071